'Benjamin injects his debut with an insider's satire, displaying an astute ear for authentic teenspeak and a keen eye for the detail of his heroine's ever-expanding designer wardrobe'
Ed Potton, *The Times*

'A great read, with some sharp observations on the exploitation of young models by the fashion industry'
Cosmopolitan

'*Landed* is the *Clueless* of the catwalks: all hot models, world-weary jet-setting and bipolar disorders'
Elle

GREG BENJAMIN

LANDED

Quartet Books

First published by Quartet Books in 2000
A member of the Namara Group
27 Goodge Street
London W1P 2LD

This edition published by Quartet Books in 2001

A catalogue entry for this book is available from the British Library

ISBN 0 7043 8158 3

Phototypeset by FiSH Books, London
Printed and bound in Great Britain by Cox & Wyman
Reading, Berks

Acknowledgements

Thanks to Sara, Ashley, Mom and Dad, Corey, Dot, Jess, Namejko, Nettie, Lindsay, Martha, Stella and everyone at Quartet. Here's to show that you can have your cake and not eat it too.

LANDED

POSTCARD OFF THE EDGE

I CAN'T HELP IT IF I'M HOT. PEOPLE TELL ME ALL THE time. I just don't listen. I dunno, beauty is such a burden sometimes. And please don't be all like, why are you pissing and moaning when you're gorgeous? You're so lucky, blah, blah, blah. All I'm saying is that beauty can be a double-edged sword. Totally.

So I was sitting in psych class totally drifting and all of a sudden the phone rings. Our school is so incredibly retarded. They have phones as well as intercoms in each room. Don't let that fool you, we're still the poorest county in the state, we just have money to spend on frivolous things.

My teacher is this funny-shaped little man. God, everyone thinks he's such a mo. I know he's not gay, but sometimes...it makes you wonder. So he saunters over to the phone and answers lispingly, 'Hello.' He's got this thing down pat where he stands with his legs like crossed, and his tongue flicking out of his mouth like a cobra. God, he's weird. Everyone in my class always makes fun of him.

My teacher keeps nodding and making noises for like five minutes. Then he stares at me. And I'm all like, hi, what are you doing? I mean, you can stare at me all you want if you wanna pay $3.75 for the *Seventeen* I'm in this month. Yeah, I'm a model . . . Whatever, it's cool. Getting back to Grendel. For real, that's his name, my teacher, like Grendel from *Beowulf*. I know, I know, I'm the only one who knows this reference. Not only beauty but brains too. Surprised, huh?

So I give him this look that says I'm bored, keep looking at me and I will castrate you. Finally, he gets off the phone and tells me I'm wanted in the CARES office downstairs. CARES is probably one of the biggest wastes in taxpayers' dollars next to the phones which don't make outgoing calls in our classrooms. It's this peer remediation thing where a counselor with a Sally Struther's degree tries to talk problems out. I have already been there once this year because this asshole said I tried to kill him. I'm not that psychotic. I mean, he asked me out and when I said no he clutched on to my car in some sort of melodramatic plea – and people think I'm Sarah Bernhardt. I didn't care so I started driving. I had a tanning session to go to. It's not my fault he stayed attached. So he's like bouncing on the road and I'm

Landed

all, oh shit, because I realize he's still there, so I just take a really wide turn and he rolls off to safety. He was damn lucky. That's why I hate guys in my school. They're all just total fuckwits.

So I have no idea why I'm wanted downstairs. I have no drug problem, at least not one that people are aware of. I'm not homosexual (a hot topic in the CARES room the past two years). I'm not involved with an abusive boyfriend. And I have no freaky step-person who's molesting me. I'm baffled. What could be going on?

I grab my backpack and walk out of the room. Mr Grendel asks me if I want him to sign my agenda in case anyone tries to hassle me for walking through the halls unattended. I'm like, uh, no. That's another stupid thing about my school. People aren't permitted anywhere without a spiral notebook which has a calendar in it and a place for teachers to sign their names. It's so juvenile. You'd think we were in fourth grade. I mean, I'm not still walking to the cafeteria single file with my hands held. You'd think they'd give us a little more slack.

I'm walking down the hall getting all kinds of looks. It happens all the time. Like I said, it's not my fault and by now I've just gotten used to it. I know I look really cute today. I'm wearing my Todd Oldham bootcut jeans and this really tight black sparkly BCBG top that's way too risqué for school and chunky black shoes. I admit I'm a pretty intimidating sight. The shoes have got at least a three-inch heel, so that makes me,

Greg Benjamin

what, like 6 feet 3 inches. Damn, I'm tall. But you've gotta be to be a model.

All right, so I'm in the CARES office and the first thing I notice is that I've got the woman counselor. Great. OK, see these so-called 'counselors', they couldn't help a turd decide whether or not to go down the toilet. They're so incompetent. And evidently, the older black guy, the lesser of two evils, is at lunch, so I'm stuck with this premenopausal bitch named Ms Barker. So I'm glancing around, looking detached, staring at my watch, you know, and all of a sudden I see Nicole.

Nicole is this flagrantly butch bisexual who's had a crush on me since freshman year. My God, she is so nasty. I think she was born on the ugly tree and hit every branch on the way down. I'm wondering what this whole ordeal is all about when Barker starts talking. She's like, 'I guess you know why you're here, Gwen.'

And I'm all, 'Not really, Ms Barker.' Real sweet and wholesome, like the persona of that Clinique ad I did last month.

So she goes, 'Nicole here says you've been threatening suicide because you feel she's not spending enough time with you. I know some people have a feeling of inadequacy and they need to attach on to others for support. That's called co-dependency. I'm really proud you're so candid about your relationship with Nicole, but if she doesn't want to be with you, you have to understand that.'

4

Landed

Does anyone have an extra pair of jeans, because I almost shit a brick. I start screaming, 'What the hell!!!' Oops, there goes Clinique girl. 'You white trash dyke bitch! How dare you lie and say something like that. God, you're so crazy. First of all I'm not a lesbian. Second of all even if you had a penis and the future of the world depended on our procreation I still wouldn't touch you with a ten-foot pole. Why would you lie like that?'

Barker's too shocked to speak for a few minutes. And then she says, 'Nicki, is that true?'

So Nicole gets all blubbery and starts crying, and, Jesus, I hate when men cry. She's whimpering and sobbing and saying she's really fucked up and was using this as a plea for my attention. She apologizes, and I'm like, whatever. Later, loser, ya know.

So she keeps crying and Barker's patting her back trying to console her, all the while staring at the snack machine wistfully. I just get up and go, and lo and behold it's time for lunch.

Lunch, one of three meals I don't enjoy eating. I'm not really anorexic per se but let's just say I have certain issues, body image being one of them. Every time I eat something with like 5+ grams of fat in it, I feel like I'm gonna explode. I decide to ditch lunch for the day. I'm thinking maybe I should head for my car and check my Motorola to see if any of my agents have called.

On my way out I run into Shazzar and Ashleigh. Leigh's

like my best friend completely. I've been friends with her for about three forevers. We used to play together in preschool, you know, dress up, house. Even then I was a diva. I refused to play the mother role, instead I was some sort of glam star who had a litter of chows and no visible husband or kids.

Leigh's looking cute as ever. She's got a nice figure, not quite as nice as mine, but whatchya gonna do? She's very athletic, about 5 feet 7 inches and trim. She and I both have long hair. Hers is a sort of cinnamon-brown color while mine is honey-colored with lots of blond.

I check out her outfit and say, 'Nice threads, Leigh… Abercrombie?' I swear she's almost as compulsive about clothes as I am. Abercrombie is her store. She has a platinum charge account which is billed, of course, to her rich father.

And she's like, 'Would you expect anything else?' And we all laugh. I fill them in on what's happened with Nicole and nobody believes it. We agree that she's a complete pillhead and needs to be put in a trailor-park institution. We just stand around for a while, looking great, and then Leigh announces she's gotta go meet her boyfriend Kirby for a 'lunch of their own'.

Me and Shaz are like, total slut city, huh. We laugh and she tells us she'll catch up with us later. As she's leaving, Shaz asks if I envy her. So I tell her of course I don't. I mean, granted she's got a great boyfriend, but I prefer being lusted after and not giving in to dating any of these losers. Shaz reluctantly agrees. We all know that he's like the only decent male high schooler around here. I mean, in a kingdom of blind men a one-eyed man can be king. Jesus God, is it slim pickings. And I feel bad for Shaz. I mean, she is totally beautiful in her own way. She's got waist-length red hair. I'm talking really red. And big green eyes and super-high cheekbones that really give her face that bitchy aristocratic look. She's incredibly fair too. Leigh and I call her Casper (the ghost) and Pinkeye, after this albino bunny rabbit I had when I was five. But no guys are ever into her. And I tell her, OK, sweetie, chill, who wants to go with these assholes anyway? She always feels better then, but I know it usually weighs heavily on her mind.

Yeah, so Leigh left and I go, 'Shaz, I'm checking my Motorola, you wanna come with me?'

And she bitches 'cause she's hungry and wants to eat lunch. I swear she eats like the horse she rides but still stays waif thin. She relents after I promise her we'll go to the bagel shop and skip fifth. On the way there she starts attacking me about her latest romantic conquest, Lance.

'Gwen,' she says, 'I'm telling you these boys are such dumbfucks.' Of course, Shaz, I know this, I'm thinking, but I let her continue. 'That limpdick prick Lance was supposed to call last night... did he? No! Today who do I see him with? That sophomore slut Erin. Yeah, Lance, cool! What do these guys see in these scrawny-ass tenth graders? I swear they're gonna end up as pedophiles.'

7

I let her vent. I mean, once she starts it's impossible to stop her. She goes, 'I don't even need to tell you how horny I am. I haven't gotten play in two months. I don't see how you can do it, not having a boyfriend. Shit, if I don't get any, I take the hand.'

I roll my eyes and she shrieks, 'What, you don't!'

I sigh really impatiently and say, 'Christ, Shaz, I told you, I'm not into that. Masochism is my form of self-love.'

She cracks up. My mental instability is totally a huge joke between us. Besides I have no use for guys right now. I'm on the road twentyfourseven. I don't look seventeen at all; why should I settle for someone at my school who does?

We go to my car and my Motorola's blinking. Surprise. It pisses me off that I'm not allowed to have it in school. God forbid someone has a life. I realize that the majority of trash in my school who own beepers and cellphones are using them to buy drugs or get in touch with their twenty-three-year-old drop-out boyfriends. But still, I'm special. Er, well that was my argument to Mr Leivitz, the principal. I almost made some headway. He was totally checking me out the whole time I was petitioning my case. I was allowed to have it in school for all of a day before some bitch from the Board of Ed made him revoke his decision. So now I have to go to my car between classes to check messages and find out where I'm booked and when.

The message on my voice mail is from Tyrone, my

manager at Click. He's cool, I guess. He's this really young, effeminate black guy from New York. He hooks me up with mad jobs but sometimes he can be really queeny. Like when he's having boy trouble, God, watch out. I remember this one time, he was in a real pissy mood 'cause he was dating this artist from SoHo who had just 'found' his sexuality or whatever. And Tyrone caught this guy porking his ex-girlfriend in his apartment. Talk about being screwed over, literally.

Tyrone was upset for days. I suffered totally. All of my accommodations were really shitty for the three shoots I had that week. That made me all anal. But I felt bad for Tyrone, I guess. He is a queen, but he didn't deserve that. Anyway, I think that artist is asexual now. So at least it's not Tyrone who's screwed up. That guy was trying to use sex to accentuate his art. Let's just say it wasn't selling.

Tyrone's extension is on speed dial. The phone's ringing and Tyrone answers... it's evident he's in a good mood.

'Gwen, baby, glad you called. Listen, sugar, I got the best job for you. Alberta Ferretti is kicking off Fashion Week here in the city, and she specifically requested you. This doesn't happen every day. I know your white ass is excited.' He pauses. 'Well, aren't you?'

'Umm... yeah, I guess. That's cool and everything but, uh what day is it...'cause it's my friend Shaz's birthday next week and I promised I'd help her celebrate in style.'

Translation: We're gonna get really fucked up.

'Girl, it's Wednesday, I already booked you. Don't cop out on me now. This is too big, besides I wanna show you my new side dish. Damn, I'm getting hot just thinking about him! I know you'll approve!'

'Christ, Ty, don't you ever ask me anymore? You can't just assume I can do every job that comes my way. I *am* in school still. I mean, I could have an exam or something. Plus, Wednesday is Shaz's birthday. What am I gonna do? My parents weren't too happy after my last weekend shoot in New York. You forgot to confirm my room so I had to stay with that photographer in his loft. What an oddball. At least I knew how to fend him off...'

'I don't care.' He's so stubborn. 'It took a lot of work for me to book this. Child, you're going. I have two tickets – two first class tickets – for New York next Tuesday. You're coming home Thursday. I'm not taking no for an answer.'

Jesus, first class. Yep, he's definitely getting some. Man, what should I do? Let's weigh up the options... Shaz's eighteenth... runway show. Hmm... Wait, did he say two tickets? Brainstorm.

'Ty, I'll call you back.' The wheels in my mind never stop turning. 'Shaz, we're going to New York!'

YOU DOWN WITH OCD?
YEAH, YOU KNOW ME!

MY PARENTS ARE KINDA SKETCHY ABOUT ME LEAVING my car at the airport. But I know my dad, if I leave my Benz here, he'll drive it all weekend. I am so psycho about who can drive my car. It's so sweet. I just got this new 1999 320 SI Mercedes convertible. It's silver. Leigh was all bitchy, like, why didn't you get white or whatever? And I'm like, hello, dyke-mobile. I already know way too many nasties driving the white ride. So I picked silver. Plus, silver's the color of the moon, moon equals goddess...hello, it's me driving here. I get it washed like two times a week. I know, I know, someone else takes it to the carwash. I don't set foot in there. Actually, now that I think about it, I'm gonna leave my car in the garage at my house. I'll hide the keys. You never know what'll happen to it at the airport. Especially with Y2K coming.

Shut up, I know it's not for like nine months but still. I'm so phobic it's recockulous. Recockulous? OK...worse than rediculous, recockulous, c'mon now. Yeah, I'm agoraphobic, xenophobic, uh...I get panic attacks in addition to my regular heightened anxiety level, I've Obsessive Compulsive Disorder (OCD), I'm anorexic (shh, don't tell), depressed and bipolar. Just commit me now, Bellevue's waiting. But that's so another story and I'm trying to tell you about New York.

I have the biggest surprises planned for Shaz. Well, first of all we tried to get Leigh to come. She couldn't, er, whatever, because it was her and Kirby's sixth month or some shit. Please. She needs to grow some balls. Anyway, I think they're having problems or something. Leigh hasn't exactly been herself. Knock me over with a feather. Something lurks beneath the cheerful façade? Well, damn, I've got my own Bill and Hillary Clinton. From what Leigh says, he's certainly a nymphomaniac. So Leigh's not coming. Life's a bitch, but what can you do? We'll all go somewhere else sometime. So I get to thinking and I am like, who do I know who could help us celebrate? Bing! So I call my friends Riley and Chris, two Ford models from the Midwest. These guys are all corn fed and whatnot, and, sure enough, they're gonna be in town for Fashion Week too. This is so fucking perfect. I've known these guys forever. They're both totally chill. It's so weird. They're like polar opposites. Riley pulls mad ass. I mean, yeah, he's a hottie and all, but he can get like whatever he wants whenever. And Chris, poor Chris, I guess he just doesn't possess the charisma needed. He cannot hook up to save his life. But he's really smart and funny, just kinda shy. Shaz and he would be perfect.

As it turns out we're all staying at the Plaza (I KNOW!!!), like down the hall. Sooooo...mission for the trip. Shaz is gonna deflower herself, on her eighteenth, with Chris, if I have to hogtie her to the four-poster bed! I dunno what's gonna happen with me and Riley. I don't need any sex to further complicate my weird life. However...Anyway, before you ask, yes, me and Riley have done the nasty on more than one occasion, although we're friends strictly speaking. Er, friends with benefits. But we'll see what happens. Or what doesn't depending on my mood.

Shaz is gorgeous. I told you that. But recently she's been looking kinda rough. So being the friend that I am, I scheduled a day of beauty for us at Bumble and Bumble Salon. Totally unselfish, I know! I'm just getting touched up, but Shaz is going through major reconstruction. Total makeover to celebrate her metamorphosis into womanhood. Hah, like so many butterflies. Never mind, inside joke.

In addition, I got us a quarter ounce of Acapulco Gold. So it's all good. She is gonna totally flip. Plus, knowing her neuro- and cardiologist parents, she'll have a platinum Visa to use at her discretion at Saks and Bloomie's. So it's gonna be one awesome trip, lemme tell you. I'm totally psyched.

I decide to take a taxi to the airport. OK, OK, a limo. I have to be wined and dined, it's a complex I have. Plus, we need the additional stretch space for all the stuff we're taking. I mean, my pharmaceuticals take up a bag of their own. I've only got four suitcases. I packed frugally because we're only gonna be gone three days. Meanwhile Shaz comes out with all of the Calvin Klein spring collection in about five different bags. I am a little annoyed, not because she brought so many clothes but because I didn't.

She's all decked out in this funky sage-colored top and embroidered flowery flare pants by Anna Sui, and I'm dressed in a black sheath dress by Chanel. We look exceptionally good. As soon as Shaz gets in I put up the glass partition, and she goes, 'Well, if this doesn't feel like *Driving Miss Daisy*.' And I say, 'Shit, Jessica Tandy never looked this good!' We both laugh.

To kick things off we decide to have a little pre-game before we fly. I suggest some Crystal but Shaz announces it's too passé. So we go with the tried and true – Lemon Drop Shooters. Luckily, Shaz has a handle of Citron in her carry-on so we can start pounding. All the while I'm thinking no wonder Shaz is a fucking genius. Now we have something to snack on in case a stewardess gets all bitchy and won't serve us. I almost have a crisis and get lemon juice on my dress, but luckily it splashes on the leather upholstery instead.

So we reach the airport and it takes five guys including this nasty thirty-five-year-old I see when I work out to lug in our stuff. This guy hits on me twentyfourseven. I may almost be eighteen but it's still illegal in my book. So they all drag our shit in there and we have about five minutes to board. We usually get there with about a half an hour to kill but I guess Shaz and I spent a little too much time doing shots. Oh, well.

Anyway, we're at the terminal and this stupid hag sporting a Worthington ensemble from J.C. Penny's tries to give me and Shaz a load of shit for taking two carry-on bags a piece. I calmly try to explain to her that my new Prada bag is considered a purse, not a carry-on. And Shaz is all, let me handle this. So she starts going on to this woman about the fascist ways of US Air. She's basically calling this woman the eastern shore's version of Joseph Stalin when they finally let us in. See, diplomacy always works.

When we take off our sunglasses and walk on the plane there's all this bustle. I guess people recognize me. I just keep my head up and do my best runway walk right up to first class with Shaz following swiftly behind. Shaz is making some comment about thank God we're here and not there because coach is just too plebeian. We're both pretty hammered by now. And I scream when the airplane goes up, having temporarily forgotten my fear of flying. Erica Jong for this generation, tell me about it. Shaz calms me down and asks if I need a Xanax and I politely decline.

I'm in a pissy mood sort of because this is a commuter plane to BWI airport and then I remember that commuter planes don't have first class. So all this while me and Shaz thought we were living the high life we were really in the section specifically designed for people over a hundred. I cannot tell you how glad I am when we land in Baltimore. We hop out of our seats and practically skip down the stairs and into the airport.

We have an hour layover so Shaz suggests we get something to drink and I think that's a novel idea. I tie my hair up in an Hermès scarf and suggest that Shaz does the same. I tell her we wanna appear incognito. We go to the bar and order Sex on the Beaches and we get carded! I'm indignant but hand my card over and both Shaz and I pass. This dampens my excitement significantly. I'm forced to drink more to get out of this mood. After three more rounds we're a little full and I suggest we prank call Leigh.

Shaz uses her cellphone, not wanting to take off her scarf and mess up her hair, hits *67 and then dials Leigh's number. She can barely stop laughing so I pinch her and then Leigh picks up. Shaz, in a nasal voice, asks for Mike Hunt. This is our favorite pseudonym since like sixth grade where we were the only ones in the school, including the principal (he sure didn't), who knew what a cunt was.

Leigh knows it's us but goes along anyway and says that Mike's not in, but his Aunt Flo's in town and would we like to speak to her? And then Shaz says she can't because Flo always makes her see red. And then I pick up the phone and say something about douching before we all crack up over our vaginal humor.

So Leigh's like, how much have you had? And I can't remember. And then I realize it's Tuesday and ask her what she's doing home from school. She corrects me and tells me it's after three and school's out and why don't I ever wear a watch?

I respond by saying that a watch doesn't really go with my outfit and what's her problem? We're both just joking and we just shoot the shit and find out what's going on. Leigh says my history teacher doesn't understand why I miss so much school. And then I'm like, did you tell her I don't understand why she has such a fat ass? And Leigh laughs and says no 'cause I was too busy laughing at her outfit. Evidently she was wearing some hideous floral muumuu. Don't ask.

Just then I hear our plane being called so I tell Leigh we'll call from New York and then we board the plane. This time there's a first class, thank God, so me and Shaz meander up there and take a seat. The plane takes off and I'm quite calm. Shaz insists we do tequila. I tell her I can't be bothered and I really don't wanna throw up on my Steve Maddens. So she sulks but ends up ordering two anyway and then drinking mine. We're just surrounded by poshness and I start to nod off and the next thing I realize, WE'VE LANDED!!

NEW YORK, HERE WE CUM

THE STEWARDESS COMES BY AGAIN AND GIVES US THESE HOT
towels for our face. Thank God, because I'm sure I look a sight.
I go in the bathroom and reapply my makeup while Shaz is
giving herself a facial with the steam from the towel.

JFK is just as I remembered, dirty. All around us people are
swarming like locusts speaking a thousand different languages.
I'm trying to find our driver from the car service but there's no
one in sight.

Shaz finally spots some guy over by baggage claim with a
sign around his neck saying 'Gwen Bendler'. We locate our
stuff, which surprisingly is all here, and follow him out to his
car with porters in tow. My feet are fucking killing me from the
heels on these things, but I'm not about to wear Easy Spirits,
or SAS like my grandmother. The guy sees me stopping every

so often to grab my foot and he says, 'C'mon, girlie, I ain't got all day.'

I know, I know this is so clichéd. He's got this exaggerated Brooklyn Italian accent. He's wearing this God-awful polyester shirt and dick-tight Gitano jeans. I was expecting a Members Only jacket but maybe we caught him on a bad day. So I give him a bitchy glare and say, sorry, I'm pigeon-toed, do you know a good podiatrist? For some reason he shuts up and we finally get to his car.

Shaz is still a little tipsy. I just have a headache. The car smells of sweat, cigarettes and designer impostor perfume. Shaz laughs and is saying something about how bohemian this is and I'm like, well, this is a little too rustic for my tastes. I'm surprised at how awful the car smells but I do remember, unfortunately, how many stars wear Elizabeth Taylor's White Diamonds. Luckily, the driver is quiet and Tyrone already told him where we were going, etc. We roll up to the hotel and we get out and grab our stuff. He tries to harangue us for a tip, but I know Ty has already taken care of everything. So I tell him my tip is to take a shower, and he does some Italian symbol for fuck you. I'm like, whatever, asshole, and me and Shaz go to check in.

The Plaza is gorgeous. Everything around us just reeks of class and money. I can tell you it's a hell of a lot better than the stench of the taxi. We get the keys to our room and take the elevator to the fourteenth floor. They're all so nice here. We just parked our shit with the receptionist and she told us a bell-hop would be up in a minute with everything.

Shaz and I cannot believe our room. It's so big! The carpet is beige and six inches thick. I could eat off it, not that I'm planning to, but if the desire arises, it's a possibility. There are two huge queen-size beds covered with pillows and soft floral blankets. We've got a TV, a Jacuzzi, a couch and a chaise-longue, a wet bar (hell, yeah!) and adequate closet space to accommodate our expansive wardrobes. Shaz makes a crude remark about creaming her panties and I laugh because I still haven't told her about the rest of her birthday, and what she said may very well happen.

Somebody's knocking on our door and there's some English guy with all our stuff and Shaz and I are very polite. You have to be around the English. I tip him heavily and he slips me his number. I'm like, eeww...and Shaz goes, 'C'mon, Gwen, he wasn't half bad.' And then I say, 'Christ, Shaz, if you think he's hot wait'll you see Riley and Chris.'

Oops.

'What are you talking about, Gwen?'

'Uh, well, I didn't tell you about your other birthday gifts, now did I?' I fill her in on what's happening with the guys.

She is screaming and jumping up on the bed and dancing around and shit. No, at this point neither of us has had any crack, she just gets like this at times. That's why I call her

ADD. She finally settles down and we decide to call Leigh, and, surprise, she's out with Kirby.

Then Shaz goes, 'How much longer do you give 'em?'

'Who, Riley and Chris, or Leigh and Kirby?'

'Bob and Elizabeth Dole, you dumbfuck, who the hell do you think!!'

'My bad bitch, take some Midol. I dunno, Leigh's happy but something seems up, y'know. I think Kirby's cheating on her.'

'Shut up, are you serious?'

I roll my eyes. 'Yeah...Look, I was at this party last Saturday at Joel's, when you and Leigh had your volleyball tournament in Delaware, and I walked in on Melissa "Growth" Anderson giving him a b.j.'

'Ohmigod, and you didn't tell her?'

'You know how she can be, Shaz. I bitched out Kirby and told Melissa she wasn't a hoover so stop sucking before she gave him an STD. Kirby got up and was like shaking and talking about how drunk he was and please don't tell Leigh. I was like, I care about her too much to say anything, Kirby, just right now I can't even look at you.'

'What did he do?'

'He turned around and pulled up his boxers. I'm serious, I couldn't keep a straight face with his two-inch whipped out, just blowin' in the wind.'

Shaz burst out laughing. 'You're shitting me.'

Landed

'I shit you not.'

So she gets all pensive-looking and is like, what should we do?

'I'm not doing anything, at least not right now. You've gotta tell her, she's not gonna want to hear it from me.'

'Why not?'

'Look, Shaz, I just can't bring myself to tell her. I'd feel all gross. I mean, can you imagine if you saw your best friend's boyfriend with some skank's mouth attached to his dick? I will talk to her, just not right away.'

Shaz is all resigned and is like, OK. Conversation is kinda halted and we just sit there a while. It's about eight o'clock and we're not doing shit, so I suggest we shower and check out the New York scene. Shaz is all worried because although it's a Tuesday, it's Fashion Week, and she doesn't see how we're gonna get a reservation anywhere, and she's all tired, blah blah.

So I'm like, fine, let's just chill here in our pajamas, watch some TV and talk to Leigh when she gets back. After all, it is Shaz's birthday tomorrow.

I take a bath and it's awesome. My hair's up in this dookey bun, and Shaz is taking it out and braiding it, and we're sitting watching movies, flicking back and forth, cracking up at the adult channel. It feels just like when we were twelve when we spent the night at Shaz's old house and found that stack of *Playboys* in her brother's room.

Shaz mutes the TV and we start making up the lines for our own porn. She's like, I'll be the guy, you be the girl, er, wait, for this scene we need two girls and a talking dildo, wait a few minutes. So we wait until the 'shower scene' is over and some thirtyish guy with a crew cut and this plastic blond with enormous breasts appear.

'Damn,' I say. 'Those are some tig old bitties!'

'Shut up,' Shaz laughs, 'we're starting.'

GWEN AND SHAZ'S NASTY PORN

S: Elizabeth, I've had a hard day at the office, do you mind sucking me off?

G: Yes, John, I do. I'm tired. I had to jog today and my gigantic tits gave me a backache. If you can guess my bra size, I'll give you head.

S: OK, 38M.

G: Well, aren't you Nostradamus? Hold on, lemme get my knee pads. (*Bends down, while he whips it out. Starts sucking.*)

S You know, Elizabeth, your tits are fucking huge!

G: (*In between sucks.*) I'm quite aware of that. (*Camera focuses in on her chest and then her mouth.*)

Aside Shaz says, 'OK, that's a prosthetic. Please, Marky Mark's in *Boogie Nights* was more realistic-looking.'

S: I had a good day at the office today. The Dow's up 26 points. No wait (*begins convulsing*) – 27, no 28, 30!!!! (*Guy comes.*)

G: You've been eating more fruit, haven't you? (*Scene changes.*) (*The End. Applause.*)

So we're both cracking up. And I have to admit we've had a fun night. It is cool to veg once in a while and to forget about being haute couture for a few minutes. So we're all in post-coital bliss when the phone rings. It's Leigh.

'Hello, Gwen and Shaz's Supercool Shagging Suite.' I laugh.

'Gwen, it's Leigh.' She sounds really upset.

'Hey, honey, what's up?'

'Kirby and me, we . . . broke up.' She begins sobbing.

'Aw, baby, what happened? I thought it was your anniversary.'

'It was, it is. I don't know. He told me it wasn't me, it was him. And that he loved me but he needed some time to himself right now. And he wanted some space. He said he felt himself growing apart from me.'

'What? I know something he's with that's got some growth!'

Oh shit, I really need to learn to shut my mouth.

'Huh?' She's sniffling. 'What do you mean?'

'Umm...I'm so sorry for you, sweetie. Here's Shaz.' I motion for Shaz to tell her.

'Sorry, Leigh honey, Gwen has the shits.'

I flip Shaz off and whisper for her to tell her. So Shaz starts talking and I can hear Leigh's voice from across the room.

'What the *fuck*, Shaz!!!! I will castrate that bastard. How could he?!!!?' (Sobbing in the background.)

Finally, after about an hour of consolation we have Leigh semi-placated. She's not mad at me and we all agree something must be done to Kirby and then to Rat Whore Melissa. We tell Leigh we love her and then hang up.

Shaz and I are emotionally and physically exhausted. We've gotta get up ass early tomorrow. My show's not until eight at night, but I have fittings starting at four and our spa thingy starts at ten. So we climb in our beds and in a matter of minutes konk out.

CATWALK'S MEOW

DESPITE BEING REALLY TIRED, I KEEP WAKING UP EVERY so often and checking the time. I have this thing where I can't sleep somewhere else besides my own bed. Yeah, it's great considering how frequently I'm on the road. It is advantageous considering I always forget to order a wake-up call. I get up at seven and take a long, hot shower. No, in case you're wondering, I did not use the complimentary shampoo and conditioner et al. Although this is the Plaza, they still don't carry Texture Line. I decide to let my hair air-dry curly, being that I pulled a muscle the last time I tried to dry my hair in a rush. I wake up Shaz and she's in a pissy mood because she says she hasn't gotten her obligatory five hours of sleep. I find that hard to believe, considering she is the worst procrastinator ever and is up half the night doing work anyway.

She takes her sweet time getting ready and at about ten to nine we're ready to get going. We decided to dress down today, so as not to appear showy. I'm wearing Urban jeans and a skimpy white Vera Wang tank. Shaz is sporting this ice-blue three-quarter-length top by French Connection and a pair of pale khaki capris. We venture down to the dining area to get our complimentary breakfast, both still kinda groggy from lack of sleep.

Luckily, all the yuppy Wall Streeters are in their offices already and the dining room is fairly empty. The waitress comes and we both know what we want. I get a bowl of strawberries and some water to wash down my Zoloft and Shaz gets a coconut scone. The service is really good, which is to be expected considering we are like the only ones besides some random Talbots-type in the restaurant. Shaz is wolfing her scone and I'm laughing and calling her a heifer and she actually takes offense. She's all, not everyone looks like they're home fresh from Dachau, Gwen. And I'm like, easy, crusher, you look like Calista Flockhart on a thin day.

I'm just joking. So she apologizes because she has not yet had her morning cup of coffee.

I have renounced coffee. The only time I drink it is when it's used as a flavoring. Like Kahlua's good and I drink Irish coffee on occasion. Supposedly, it's really bad for your teeth. Besides, too many people I know are already strung out on stuff from Colombia, wait…that's cocaine. Still, I'm anxious enough as it is. Even Sanka would make me jumpy.

We don't wait for the waitress to return, just leave some money on the table, trusting Shaz's implicit math ability to calculate a fair tip. Bumble and Bumble is about four blocks away so we decide to hike it since we have no idea what kind of taxi we might encounter.

Shaz almost fainted when I told her about our, er, actually her, makeover. She has been dying for one for the longest time. The people in the salon are really good. The first time I went in there I was so nervous since most of the stylists had haircuts resembling neo-Nazis. But my hair is exquisite and ass-long and they said they wouldn't touch it. So we get there in about five minutes; bear in mind Shaz and I are volleyball players and have incredible speed, agility and stamina. Shaz has never been to a really trendy, minimalist salon, so she was pretty taken back.

First, we're introduced to Ilena, who's our esthetician. She took us to some private room and we had to strip and be covered with this mud mixture. I made some off-color joke to Shaz about female wrestling and Ilena seemed pretty irritated. I shut up. I hate those bitchy, punk New York types! Then we shower off and get some sort of loofah scrub which supposedly exfoliates with sea salts. I'm like, I don't wanna come out of here smelling like the Dead Sea, so they took it easy on me.

Then Ilena gives us to Trish and Luc, who are the massage therapists. Luc's a hardbody and Shaz so wants him to do her, but I inform her that he's gay, so don't get your panties in a bundle. She didn't care. She practically had an orgasm when he did her lower back. Next, we've got haircuts, color and final rinse. My stylist is Choi, this Korean American who lives in SoHo. She is definitely the coolest Korean I know. We decide to give me a gold rinse to shine up my highlights. I just end up getting a trim and my cut is more angular. It looks great though. Shaz goes through this complete metamorphosis.

Her hair now hangs three inches below her shoulder. She had a lot chopped off. Her red hair is now this rich brown color with these bronze and copper highlights throughout. It's all layered around her face and it looks incredibly diva. I'm like, hell, yeah, Shaz, you look great. She loves it, I can tell.

We pay for everything and jet. It's almost two now, so I totally have to haul ass to my fitting. I give Shaz her ticket and tell her where and when to go for the show. She's off to shop for the duration of the day. Lucky cow. I take a taxi to somewhere on Madison and eventually find my way to the building. Inside's a madhouse. Models are everywhere and all these stylists are running around making alterations and tugging at everything. I pop two Xanax for good measure.

'Gwen, darling, come here!' I turn around and see Mika, a

friend of mine who I usually do runway with. I give her a hug and she fills me in on her gossip.

'God, it's been such a long time since I've seen you.' Not long enough. Mika's not really my friend. In fact, I can't stand her. She's this whorish, waif-like model with a stick up her ass. We're both the youngest models here which is weird 'cause usually there's some thirteen-year-old prepubescent who looks like she just returned from a sweat shop.

Mika is trying to talk to me, but luckily a heavy-set woman with a British accent comes over and starts making me try on clothes. My Xanax is kicking in so the rest of the afternoon is kind of uneventful. I have three outfits in the first twenty minutes which isn't too bad. In the second part, I have five, three of which are evening gowns, and that makes it kind of a bitch. I'm pissed because I have to wear stilettos which make me like 6 feet 5 inches, so I feel like the Jolly Green Giant. I convince the stylist to let me wear ballet flats with two of the dresses, which means I have to wear the dreaded heels only once.

At eight o'clock all the doors are shut and Alberta comes out and says a few things. Everyone around me is rather nonchalant. Most of the models are staying for the rest of the week doing shows for Issey Miyake, Prada, Gucci and Bill Blass. I'm thrilled this is the only show I'm doing because I need to catch up with school. Cringe.

Techno starts pumping and the show begins. I walk out there

strutting my stuff and I can tell all eyes are on me. I really work it. I can see Shaz laughing at me and I'm pretty sure she's sitting next to Riley and Chris. Damn, I'm thinking, she certainly wasn't shy with them. I start playing situations out in my mind and I almost trip, so I just keep concentrating on walking.

The show goes well. I have no desire to party afterwards with a lot of these substanceless models. So immediately after it's over, I grab Riley, Chris and Shaz and we hail a taxi and get out of there.

Chris gives me a big hug and Riley pretends he's gonna kiss my cheek and then grabs my face and tongues me. All of them start cracking up and I'm like, whoa, hotrod, take a chill. Both of them look good. They're friends sort of the way me and Shaz are. They grew up together and played sports and whatever. Right after high school they tried their hand at modeling and got signed by Ford. They're two years older than us but it's all good.

Riley's got his hair cropped really short and all messed up and Chris's is kinda in one of those 'I just woke up' styles. Chris and Shaz are already holding hands…I guess Riley filled him in on my plan.

They've all eaten. I, like usual, am not hungry so now we've gotta figure out what to do. They're all insisting on clubbing and I consent, although usually it's not my scene. So we go to some popular rave scene where Riley knows the bouncer and we get in immediately and aren't even carded.

Landed

Chris and Shaz are kind of just standing around awkwardly, so me and Riley tell them to wait there and we make a beeline to the bar. Riley puts his arm around me as we're walking and it's just like old times. We've got a really cool friendship and can just pick up from wherever we've left off. We get to talking and he starts saying how he's missed me and all and I'm like, aw, that's so sweet, but easy, 'cause I doubt you're getting any. He gets all serious and goes shit, and then we both crack up and say, 'Just joshing,' at the same time. He eyes me seductively but then our drinks come.

We walk back to where Shaz and Chris were standing and see them doing some pretty raunchy freaking. I bust out laughing and me and Riley down our shots (and theirs too) and then join them. We all do a freak train and after a while I'm tired so I suggest, or rather demand, that we sit down.

Everybody is kinda out of breath and the scene is starting to get kind of sketchy with all the club kids entering so we leave and head back to our room. In the taxi I call shotgun, why I don't know, and Riley sits in the back sulking. Shaz has her head on Chris's shoulder and I groan and say, look at the married couple already. Shaz gives me the bird and I say, sit and spin. She just puts her head back where it was and kisses his neck.

I'm like, easy now, we don't wanna get this too steamy, and then Riley goes, 'Yeah, that's for later.'

Everybody cracks up and is in a really good mood. Riley

takes care of the cab fare and we all go back to the room. Our room is immaculate enough even to suit my obsessive compulsive tastes. Chris, Riley and Shaz sit down on the beds while I play bartender. Mid-pour I realize that I haven't wished Shaz a happy birthday so I turn around and tackle her and scream, 'Happy birthday!'

Riley informs us that if we stay in that position he'll have to go the bathroom for ten minutes and I inform him, 'No, it'll be more like two.' I try to give Shaz eighteen spanks when Chris goes, 'Don't worry, Gwen, I'll take care of that later.'

I'm like hell, yeah, Chris, now you're talking. Shaz is a little red but I tell her to ease up. We start drinking and laughing and I totally forget about my bag of weed. I'm about to go get it when Riley goes, 'Hey, how about we play Truth or Dare.'

I groan. He's so horny. This is just his excuse to get us to take off our clothes. But Shaz is all for it and Chris grins and says he doesn't care, but it's obvious he wants to. I say, fine, it's not like you all haven't seen my titties. So Riley says he'll start and here's our game.

SHAGADELIC TRUTH OR DARE

R: (*With mischievous grin*) Chris, truth or dare?

C: (*Looking sheepish*) Truth.

Landed

All: PUSSY!!!!

R: No, guys, it's OK. Chris, do you have a boner right now?

C: (*Turning red*) Shut up, man.

R: I take it that's a yeah?
(*Chris gets redder, shakes his head.*)

G: Riley, you're an asshole, you know that? Nope, that's not my question, no rhetoric. Shaz, truth or dare?

S: (*Already buzzing*) Uh, dare.

G: Confirm Riley's question.

S: (*Shrugs, reaches over and grabs Chris*) Yep, answer confirmed.
(*Everybody laughs, Chris relaxes.*)

S: Riley, truth or dare?

R: Dare, of course. (*Puts hand on fly.*)

S: Whip it out.
(*Riley does so.*)

G: If this is gonna be an exhibition show we might as well just get naked now.

R: (*Eagerly*) You want to?

G: Riley, come here. Shaz, don't you have something, um, to take care of. C'mon, Riley, let's see how the Jacuzzi's working. (*Drags him up and walks into bathroom, closes door.*)

C: Happy birthday, Shaz. (*Walks over and tentatively kisses her.*)

S: Let's make it even happier. (*Pulls him towards her.*)

Mission accomplished.

After we all got that out of our systems, I got out my bowl and we do up the reefer. Damn, that stuff is strong. After five hits I'm gone. Shaz is already in a euphoric state, so she only does like two, and Riley and Chris do eight apiece. Everybody is in the best mood. The phone rings but nobody feels like answering it. The machine picks up and it's Leigh.

'Hey, guys, guess you're out. I hope your show went well, Gwen. Thanks for the talk last night, I feel much better. I'm still really upset at the male species in general, but I think I'll make it until you guys get back. Anyway, I'm going to bed now so don't call back but I'll pick you all up at the airport tomorrow at five. Ciao.'

Riley's kinda curious. 'Who was that?'

'Oh, that's Shaz's and my best friend, Leigh. She and her boyfriend broke up last night and we had to tell her the real reason.'

'Which was?'

'He was cheating on her. I walked in on some slut giving him head.'

'Ouch.'

Landed

'Yeah, I know. She's such a sweetie. She deserves so much better.'

'Is she hot?'

'Asshole. Is that all you think about?'

'I'm joking.' Riley turns serious. 'No, because we have a friend who just broke up with his girlfriend and he's looking to meet somebody.'

'I dunno, it's kinda soon afterwards. Plus, when is she gonna meet him?'

'Well, that's what I wanted to talk to you about. Me and Chris, we were talking while you and Shaz went to get ice. We wanted to do something different this summer. Live at the beach, get a normal job, chill, you know? And you all live right by the beach. Didn't you live there last summer?'

'Yeah, so . . .'

'So we've actually been thinking about this for a really long time, and we're gonna live at the beach this summer.'

'No shit! That's awesome.' I give him a big hug. 'Well, what did you want to talk about?'

'We wanna get a place that's pretty big . . .' He grins. 'Do you know three good-looking people who might wanna room with us?'

I smile back. 'I could think of some.'

The next morning we all get up late and go to a coffee shop

diner for breakfast. Everybody showers at our place. This time I get up ass early so I have time to dry my hair. It's kind of chilly so I put on my drawstring jeans from Abercrombie and this stretch cardigan by Cousin Johnny. Shaz is just wearing jeans and a Lucky sweater. I told you we were underdressed. The guys wear what they wore last night.

At the coffee shop the guys order these lumberjack breakfasts and Shaz gets waffles. I have herbal tea. Shaz looks over at me, shakes her head, and her eyes get real big in pantomime, 'You sure you're gonna be able to eat all that, Porky?' And I just give her this weary look. I haven't taken my meds yet so I'm kind of in a grouchy mood. Chris picks up the bill, what a sport, and we head back to our hotel.

Again our place is exceptionally clean. We finish packing our stuff with Riley and Chris's help and then check out of the hotel. On the way to the airport, Shaz is crying and Chris is holding her and even Riley, who usually is macho as hell, looks upset. I'm like, you guys better come visit soon. And they promise and Shaz and Chris exchange numbers and addresses and everything. I give Riley a hug goodbye. And Shaz and Chris are kissing forever.

We wave as we board the plane and Shaz looks chagrined as we melt into our seats. 'Thanks for everything, sweetie. I had the best birthday.'

'Hey, what are friends for?' I smile.

Landed

The plane takes off and this time I don't scream. The city gets smaller as we ascend. We're both pretty upset. The stewardess comes by and asks us if we'd like anything to drink in the interim.

I look at Shaz. 'Please,' we both say, 'whatever it is, make sure it's a double.'

NEEDED HIATUS

I GET HOME AND I'M EXHAUSTED. MY PARENTS, LIKE USUAL, are really curious about the runway show and my goings-on in New York. I fill them in on what happened. Not everything. Yeah right. I invent some tale about how Shaz and I spent last night, but I do mention that we hung out with Riley and Chris.

My parents absolutely adore the two of them. I guess it's because they're such brown-nosers. They are all about knowing what they're up to and whatever. So I tell them about the whole beach idea and they actually don't seem bothered. I don't give my parents justice. Sometimes they're really cool. Both are ex-hippies and are incredibly laid back. Basically, if I'm a good person they let me do anything. They know I've made good on myself and that I wouldn't intentionally do anything to cause myself harm. On second thoughts, maybe they don't know me too well. I have been known to have self-destructive tendencies.

I fall asleep as soon as I hit the pillow, which is a relief since I'm running low on Seconals. The next thing I know it's 5.42 and I'm climbing out of my loft to start my day. Thank God for Fridays. I shower for thirty-five minutes. I fall asleep in there like only twice and then towel dry and put in a hair mask. I get dressed in my pjs and proceed to do my 650 morning crunches. Don't be surprised; I told you I was compulsive. After my stomach's toned, I ground myself and meditate, kinda channel my energy and focus on the upcoming day. The light's shining from my window already. Oh man ... it's beautiful out, and I've gotta be in school. Or do I?

It's gonna be in the low to mid-60s I think, so I put on a TSE linen dress and a raw silk cardigan over the top. I don't have the energy to dry my hair so I let it go curly and go downstairs. My parents are still sleeping, lucky bastards. I get a glass of orange juice, take my pills and grab an Evian for the road.

I start driving to school and get to thinking. You know, fuck this, I can't be bothered. I'll catch up with Leigh tonight. I drive past school and head out to Route 50 and start towards the beach. I figure, my parents said they're cool with me living there again for the summer. I might as well start apartment hunting.

I get all nostalgic about the beach and I realize I haven't

talked to my friend Sandee in ages. Sandee is this neurotic Italian woman I worked with who moved down from Pittsburgh twenty-five years ago. She's a trip. She's average height, about 5 feet 4 inches, and stick skinny. She's got this faded red hair that must be some forgotten shade of Clairol. She has got to be the funniest woman I've ever met. She chain-smokes like a goddamn chimney and does a little reefer on the side to mellow out. She's about as anxious as I am. It figures, she lives on coffee and Newports. Who wouldn't be jittery?

I call her. I'm certainly not worried about waking her, Christ, she's up at five o'clock every day. She doesn't answer the phone till the fourth ring.

'Hello.'

'Sandee, what's up, *chica*? It's Gwen. How's it going?'

'Gwennie. Uh, what the hell's happening?' I can tell she's smoking.

'Not a whole lot. I'm taking a little hiatus from school. Just got back from a runway show last night. I figured, who gives a shit, right? So I'm apartment hunting today at the beach. You wanna meet me for lunch somewhere? Or at least a cup of coffee?'

'Oh, Jesus. You better get the hell outta here. Vince's car's in the shop. He's driving mine. How the fuck am I gonna get over there?' I love it she cusses as much as I do.

'Sandee, that's bullshit. His car is fine. In your last e-mail you told me he just got a new car. You can't let him be so possessive over you and tell you where you can go every five minutes. He's treating you like shit. Don't take it.'

'I know!! I'm leaving his ass. Yesterday, I saw that bitch Linda, that internet whore he's been seeing, I saw her name up on his ICQ, you know. So I says, "Listen, Vince. You need to stop writing that homewrecker. Both of you are married and I'm gonna tell her husband."'

'And what did he say?' I'm trying not to laugh but she gets so passionate about her philandering husband and his internet conquests.

'He said I'm full of shit. I told him he better get the hell out. I swear to God I almost packed my bags. My cousin's a divorce lawyer, ya know. So then I figured he woulda liked that, so I told him I was gonna fix both their asses. I oughta piss on that goddamn computer!'

I busted out laughing. 'Sandee, you're too much. Listen, I'll meet you at Polock Johnnie's at one. See ya, babe.' Click.

I know she's probably sulking and saying she won't come. Probably getting herself all worked up. But she'll be there. Sandee is one reliable chick. I can always count on her.

In the interim, I decide to page Shaz and Leigh and leave them a voice mail telling them what's up. It's nice just to cruise with my sunroof down, just chilling, driving while the sun beats down. Oh, I should've worn a hat. My stylist gets really bitchy about sun-damaged hair. Ah, screw it.

Greg Benjamin

I get to the beach around nine and cruise down the south of Ocean City checking out what's available. There's a whole lot of shit is what there is. But one place catches my eye. It's this huge, white, Victorian house on the bay behind North Division Street. It's three bedroom (plus), two bathroom (bigger plus) and has a huge deck for mad parties. I'm so sold. I write down the number and address of the house, all warm and happy from my find.

Before I continue, I'm sure a lot of you are wondering, what I, Gwen Bendler, high-price fashion model, am doing in some crummy little beach town. Easy, I was getting there. There's gotta be some kind of dichotomy to my life. I can't be glamorous on every day of the week. I need my summers to recuperate. So usually, well, at least since I was thirteen, I've lived on my own in Ocean City. Don't be so shocked. My parents trust me. I haven't gotten in trouble with the police, save that one time, and it's been a building experience. Besides, I need some time without parental supervision to try and regain my sanity.

By the time I've finished it's almost one. Damn, I must've been looking hard. I park my car in a metered lot and start walking towards Polock's. Sure enough I see Sandee in khaki jeans and a sweatshirt, standing outside smoking a cigarette and looking indignant.

'Where the hell have you been?' she asks.

Landed

'Christ, Sandee, it's only five of one right now.'

'Oh, well, I thought it was later. So what's going on?'

We go inside, take a booth and order our usual: small Cokes which we don't finish. I harp on Sandee about her eating habits so I figure I should try to set an example. I get a salad and Sandee, to my surprise, get's a corndog. I have to laugh because she's always bitching about how they give her indigestion.

It's great to see her. We catch up on work gossip and what's been going on otherwise. I fill her in on the runway show and what's been happening with Riley, Chris and Shaz. I even tell her about Leigh and Kirby. Sandee is very sympathetic. She's only met Leigh twice but she loves her. Plus, if it involves a cheating lover, Sandee's always interested. She tells me to tell Leigh to fix the bastard. My sentiments exactly.

It's almost 2.30. We've been talking forever. I pay since she always insists on treating and go back to my car. I miss Sandee so much. It'll be great seeing her on a daily basis. I call the number and leave my name and a message. I'm sure that house will be ours. I got a good feeling from it. On my way back to town I get to thinking about what Sandee said about Kirby: 'Fix the bastard.' Hmm...maybe we should. After all, what else is there to do on a Friday night in our deadass town?

I'm so glad I wore this cardigan. I am now convinced that all the weather forecasters in the world are on crack. Actually, I take that back, I don't know about Al Roker on *Today*. All the local ones don't have a clue. It's only like 44 degrees out and I really don't feel like putting the heat on in my car. I'm sorry, it's sacrilege to put on heat when it's almost April. It's all good. I'll just shiver on my way back to town. Maybe I can burn some calories that way. Fuck me. That's a reminder. I haven't been to the gym in two days. Okay, Gwen, don't flip out, just go as soon as you get home. Luckily for me I keep a set of gym clothes in my car for such dire emergencies so I don't have to go home to change.

The gym's not that crowded which is fine with me. I get anal when I can't use my machine or when somebody is using my weights in the free-weight room. I do arms, abs, chest and cardio today and I'm only in there about ninety minutes. I start feeling better too, ya know. My blood's circulating, I'm into my rhythm. All of a sudden I see Repulsive Old Man. ROM for short. ROM is this vile, pathetic, greasy old man who makes me livid. This bastard thinks he owns the Y. I can't decide which bothers me more, his fashion choice, or his odor. Granted not everyone can afford DKNY athletic garb, but that's still no reason to look bad. ROM has got these hideous sweatsuits. I would sooner work out naked than put on one of these atrocious excuses for clothing. He has two which he alternates. One is bottle-green with an apple or something embroidered on it; the embroidery boasts of some type of volunteer fire department to which he must have belonged back when they had to put fires out with their own saliva or something. The other is a burgundy, merlot-colored if you will, more form-fitting sweatsuit that depicts a place called Catlinsville. I have never heard of this place therefore it's obviously the town that God forgot.

Today ROM's wearing the green number and he glares at me as we pass. We have this mutual contempt for each other. I have no idea when it started, but he always stays on *my* machines for what seems like hours at a time. Plus, he doesn't use them properly, another reason why he should be shot. He also rests between each of his eight sets. My God, why don't we just have a respirator which can follow him around? Plus, he's sneaky. Like, whenever he gets done with a machine, he always puts the pin on some huge weight. Please, like he could even lift an economy pack of Centrum Silver, let alone 240 lb. For some reason he wants to appear hardcore. He wears this weight belt which I find hilarious since the only machine where he actually lifts something which would require it is a vertical bench machine, and again he doesn't do it properly. And for not working hard, he sweats rivers! I go through a bottle of disinfectant each time I clean up after him. Seeing him puts me in a bad mood. Luckily, I'm done with everything just as he walks in so I don't have to deal with his shit today.

When I get home, there's a note from my parents saying they're at the Giant and two messages, one from Shaz and one from Leigh. Whenever I play my machine I always like to play my recording, not because I'm self-absorbed, but just because it's so cool.

The first message is from Shaz: 'Hey, Gwen, way to cop out on classes today. Fielding was pissed. She asked me where you were, like I'm your goddamn keeper, and I told her you were probably exploring transcendentalism by going somewhere else because you didn't feel like being here. She just gave me a look and, oh, I got a fucking detention because I was late again. My fault. I know having to urinate is a vice shared by few, but still, can you cut me some slack? Whatever. Anyway, what are we doing tonight? I am in a wonderful mood because there was a message from Chris on my answering machine. I almost passed out from sheer bliss. Anyway, I'm riding until seven so page me or leave a message on my machine. Later, *chica*.'

She has no bones about leaving any sort of message on my machine. What if my parents were to hear? Wait, did you actually think I am serious? My parents think Shaz is hilarious. They'd probably hit repeat just to hear it again. Leigh's message has its usual zing too.

'Hey, Gwen, this is Leigh. Why weren't you in school? Did

Prada call and say they needed you on the runway pronto...
Kirby didn't even look at me today. Bastard must die. I'm in a
really pissy mood. To top it all off Flo came today so my week
just keeps getting better and better. I'm at home, gaining
weight as we speak. Call ASAP to prevent me from bingeing...
[pause] too late. Call me anyway.'

They're too much. I go to hit erase on my machine, but I
guess I didn't see there's another message. Man, I hope it's not
Tyrone. I need to catch up on my work with a hardcoreness.

'Uh, Gwen, hey, what's up? This is, um, Kirby. Gimme a
call when you get home or whatever. My number's 555 2515.
Maybe we can chill tonight. Later.'

OK, um...can I get a what the fuck. I knew this colder
weather was like a portent of bad stuff. I feel a deep foreboding
too. Maybe I should consult the tarot. Nah, I'll just call and
find out. The shower can wait. I dial the number.

'Hello.'

'Is Kirby there please?'

'This is him.' Wow, such inflection. Uh, no.

'Kirby, what's up? This is Gwen. Did you call?'

'Hey!' Tone changes. 'What's up?'

'Um, nada really. I was at the beach and then I went to the
Y. Did you call?'

'Wow, that's heavy. You went to the beach today? Did you
like have a shoot a something?'

'No, no shoot today. I just met a friend up there 'cause I didn't feel like going to school and I had to go apartment hunting.'

'Tight. Wait, apartment hunting? Why?'

'Oh, I'm living at the beach this summer with three guys and, hopefully, Shaz and *Leigh*. I wanted to get a good place before they were all taken.'

'Did you find one?'

I'm thrilled he's being so abundantly clear as to why he called.

'Uh, yeah, I think. It's this big white house bayside on N. Division and Chicago.'

'Heavy. But don't the cops, like, give you a lot of shit down in South OC?'

'I lived there last summer and didn't have a problem. I think it just depends.'

'Oh. [long pause] So yeah. Um, what are you doing tonight?'

'I have no fucking clue. Shaz and Leigh called and were wondering the same thing.'

'Oh.' My, he expresses his sentiments so eloquently. 'Are you, like, going to Brayden's?'

'I hadn't really thought about it. I dunno. I haven't done the whole high school scene in a while, ya know?'

'So now's your chance to get reacquainted!'

'Um...I dunno. I'll talk to Shaz and Leigh.'

'I mean, I could like give you a ride if you want?'

'Thanks, that's sweet, but you only have a two-person car.'

'I know.'

What is he getting at?

'Uh, shit, Kirby, that's my agent on the other line. I better take it. Maybe I'll see you later. OK, see ya.' Click.

Tyrone isn't on the other line. Now I'm totally bugging. What is up with this shit? I know he's not trying to get up on me. I am so not into that. Especially since Leigh just broke up with him. Please, did he think because I saw him with Melissa I was impressed? Hi, I've seen it before, and, frankly, I'm not. Leigh's gonna shit when she finds out. I better go shower.

Shaz calls me right as I'm about to get into the shower. I swear I'm gonna cramp up or, worst of all, get a zit if I don't get in the water soon. I apply a cucumber mask as I answer the phone.

'Yo.'

'Hey, bitch.'

'Hey, Shaz, what's going on? Your hymen hurting after riding all day?' Sometimes even my sense of humor repulses me.

'Heh, heh. Not really. You know how it is. Chris gave it a good workout the other day so...'

'Yeah, I do know, I heard you even with the Jacuzzi

running. Oh, incidentally, I never found out... how does everybody like your new look?'

'Everybody shat! You would not believe how many looks I got and what everybody was saying. I'm no longer Brain. It's like the true sex goddess has emerged.'

'Cool beans. What'd you wear today?'

'Um ... Navy stretch deep V-neck by Free People and khaki cargo flare pants by Bebe. You?'

'TSE linen sundress and cardigan. I was fucking freezing.'

'Where were you?'

'Oh, I went to the beach to go apartment hunting. I have found the most money place!'

'Awesome! This summer will be so phat. You're so lucky your parents just let you get up and go whenever. If mine don't let me live there this summer... Actually, there is no if. They will or it will be a double homicide.'

'C'mon, Shaz, your 'rents aren't that bad. Besides matricide is so Menendez.'

'Too true, too true. So what else is going on?'

'Listen, you're not gonna believe me if I tell you.'

'Spill it.'

'Guess who called me?'

'Joey Lawrence?'

'What the fuck? Yeah, and Blossom too. Are you on crack? I'm being serious.'

Landed

'Mine is strictly a nasal habit, dear, you know this. I'm listening, *creaming* in anticipation.'

'As only you would. OK, OK...[pause] Kirby.'

'Shut up! What did he say?'

'He likes me I think. Can you imagine his nerve? I mean, after the whole breakup with Leigh and even after I saw his, you know...in Growth's mouth. Ugh.'

'Ohmigod. I can't believe this. What did he want?'

'Besides me naked...um, to go out tonight.'

'What'd you tell him?'

'Well, supposedly, there's this party at Brayden's right. So he wanted to take me to it. I was like, I dunno. Me, Leigh and Shaz are doing something so maybe we'll see you there. Then I told him Ty was on the other line and I better go.'

'What did Tyrone want?'

'Oh, nothing. He wasn't even on. I was just bugging so bad I had to get off and fast. So, do you wanna go tonight?'

'Sure, now that I'm Aphrodite incarnate, I'd like to get all decked out and show everybody the new Shaz.'

'Nymphodite is more like it. Cool. Call Leigh. You guys come over at 7.30. We'll drink here and then go over to Brayden's around nine or so. Dress really sexy. Let's rub it into all these assholes what they're missing.'

'Cool, see ya around seven.' For Shaz that was like 7.30 to 7.45.

'OK, later.' Click.

Damn, I hope Leigh isn't too upset. Shit! This mask is starting to burn.

I take my time getting ready. I wash my hair and put extra conditioner in it so I won't have to listen to my stylist bitch about dryness 'cause I forgot to wear a hat today. After I dry off, I apply some smoothing serum and an intensive leave-in conditioner to my wet hair. I put on a bathrobe and take the time to blow it out straight. I'm trying to think of what I should wear. God, I haven't been to a high school party in forever. I can't really wear a skirt. I decide on Dolce & Gabbana low-rise flare pants that are super tight and give everybody hard-ons. I have this tight, silver midriff tank that goes really well. I leave my hair down but put a few silver clips in. I look really cute.

The doorbell rings and it's Shaz and Leigh. I guess they just took one car. Leigh's wearing boycut jeans and a tight boatneck shirt that's pale purple. I think both are Banana Republic. Shaz is wearing this fitted iridescent blue workshirt by XOXO and navy slim-fit ankle-length pants. We all look so good.

Shaz has told Leigh about my conversation with Kirby and Leigh is livid. I give her a brief 411 on what happened and she's determined to make his life hell.

'Well, how should I act towards him?' I ask her.

'I dunno. I'm thinking you should either be 100 percent tease or else totally brush him off. Either or.'

'Whatever. How are you gonna react?

'I'm thinking about being really nice to Brayden, if you catch my drift.' She smiles mischievously.

'Oh God, don't turn nympho on me now, Leigh. Please, one is enough per group.' I look over at Shaz, who gives me the finger. 'Eat me, Shaz.'

She sticks out her tongue and wiggles it.

'God, you two are so gross. Don't worry, I'm not gonna do him, yet. I was thinking of maybe having Kirby find us in a compromising position.'

'Ah, I see. Turnabout's fair play, huh?'

'Yup.'

'Well, whatever, as long as I don't have to put out. Don't mess too bad with Brayden, he's a cool guy.'

'I know, I like him. We'll see what happens. Besides I'm saving room for Riley's friend.' She grins.

God, will this be an interesting night . . .

'MATERIAL GIRL'
AND OTHER MADONNA
FAUX PAS

OF COURSE, NO ONE AGREES TO MY PLAN. I WANT TO DRIVE up in a limo and that way we can drink, but Leigh wants to be completely sober so she can watch Kirby suffer. That's fine with me and Shaz, so we begin pounding. I advise that we drink sensibly so as not to be completely shit-faced. We only do about six shots in twenty minutes and are feeling quite nice.

It's good to be with the gals. The party is all the way out in Bumfuck. Brayden lives like twenty minutes away on the other side of town. By the time we get there, there's about thirty or so cars already parked in the surrounding vicinity. I know, it's so easy to spot a high school party, but whatchya gonna do? I make Leigh park facing out which is a task all in itself. Sorry, but I really don't need any more trouble with the cops. Granted, it's not like I'll need to make a quick getaway from the paparazzi, however once again I'd like to be prepared if the need arises.

Music is blasting from inside the doors. Some sort of rap or something. Nothing I'm really familiar with. Maybe people just need a beat to dryfuck to. We all kind of dance our way in the door. People look really surprised to see us...I guess that's to be expected. But it's not as if I'm a leper or made of glass or something. I must look kind of unapproachable because everyone is trying not to stare at me and absolutely no one is talking to me. Shaz has gone off and found a chaise-longue and is sprawled out like a queen in some sort of intoxicated delirium. I'm already having a blast. Let's see, obviously I'm the life of the party, the music is courtesy of some gangsta dude, and I have this hunch someone is gonna spill cheap beer all over my shoes. Maybe not, lightning doesn't strike the same spot twice. Even better, beer goes really well with my Dolce & Gabbana. I'm flat up against a wall with my bored, detached model pose on, when I hear somebody call my name.

'Hey, Gwen.' It's Kirby. He's got this baseball cap on and he's wearing a plaid shirt and jeans. Normal high school garb. Jesus, this is gonna be awkward. 'Hey, can I talk to you for a sec?'

'Um...OK.' What am I supposed to say?

'Great.' He flashes me this toothy grin. I feel kinda bad. If he hadn't fucked around with Growth he'd be such a nice guy.

'Where to, sir?'

He motions for me to follow him and we walk upstairs into one of the bedrooms. Can this get any more clichéd. He sits down on one side of the bed and I'm all the way on the other, almost falling off. This is tricky because I'm trying to look good while maintaining delicate balance.

'OK,' he starts. 'When I called, I didn't want to give you the wrong idea. I don't have feelings for you. It may have come across that way on the phone but I wanted to talk to you about Leigh. I care about her a lot...she's a great girl. I wondered what she told you about our problems.'

Problems...? I didn't say anything. Leigh never mentioned anything being wrong in boyland.

'She did tell you we were having problems, right?' He looks at me wide-eyed.

'Um...not really, but I'll take your word for it.'

'Jesus, I can't believe she didn't tell you. The day you saw me with Melissa we had broken up, er, sorta. We both felt we needed some time to chill. I was in a really bad mood and I got totally fucked. I should never have done anything with Melissa but I wasn't making the best decisions in the state I was in.'

I smile at him. 'No shit.'

'But listen,' he continues, 'it's just that things weren't, like, meshing well between us. It was sort of my fault really. I always wanted to spend time with her and go places with her, etc. ....

But she felt I was being way too possessive. I thought I gave her plenty of space, but obviously not.'

He looks really sad. Wait a minute! Why would Leigh lie to me?

'Hold up, Kirby. What are you talking about? Leigh told us that you were breaking up with her. She never said anything about being mad.'

'Are you serious?' He looks at me incredulously.

'Yup.' I nod. I feel bad for him and I'm slightly irritated at Leigh for lying. What's up with her?

'Hold on, Kirb, I'll be right back.'

I walk down the stairs and almost break my neck tripping over this couple who seriously need to find a room. I don't see Leigh dancing or anything. Finally, I go into Brayden's downstairs bedroom and I see her sitting on his bed looking sad.

'What got up your ass, Leigh?'

'Huh? Jesus Christ, you scared me. Why aren't you dancing?'

'Yes, because there's an abundance of great-looking, sophisticated people to dance with. I was gonna ask you the same thing.'

'Oh, I'm just feeling out of it.'

'Why? You weren't drinking.'

'Oh, I know. It's just, well . . . I always used to go to these sort of things with Kirby and now that we're not together it's kind of depressing.'

'Do you see him with anybody else?'

'I doubt he's here. He probably never showed up after you said you weren't coming. Maybe he's with the girl I bet he's seeing.' She looks down at the floor.

I've had enough. I'm glad Leigh's not an actress because she'd be winning an Oscar right now.

'Come off it, Leigh. I know what really happened. I just talked to Kirby upstairs. Why'd you lie to me? He never broke up with you. I'm really hurt. I'm your best friend or at least supposed to be. What's up with lying to me like that?'

She looks shaken. 'What, what did he tell you?'

'About how you orchestrated the breakup and about your fights and everything.'

'Oh, man.' She starts crying. 'I thought you wouldn't understand. I'm really upset. It's, well, I was getting so close to Kirby and here it is senior year. And you and Shaz are leaving me next year, and, after my mom, I couldn't handle anyone else going. I wanted to distance myself so I didn't get hurt. I thought you'd be pissed at me for doing that to Kirby.'

'Aw, honey, I love you. We're not gonna grow apart. We'll see each other all the time. But I am pissed. It was fucked up what you did to Kirby and I don't like being lied to. It happens enough to me at work. But it's not my concern right now. I think you need to talk to Kirby. Who knows what'll happen in the future, besides Dionne Warwick.'

Landed

She flashes a smile.

'Anyway, I mean, if you still have feelings for Kirby, tell him. He misses you. Damn!' I push her. 'Go upstairs and talk to him, he's in the guest bedroom.'

She sniffles. 'OK, thanks.'

I give her a hug and watch her as she leaves the room. I'm so good. Meanwhile this party is getting lamer by the minute. I join Shaz on the couch in the other room while the remaining people are milling around us. I fill Shaz in but she's too drunk to care.

I decide to go check in on Leigh and Kirby. The door's locked and the light's off. I knock and call to Leigh.

'Leigh, are you almost ready to jet?'

'Um...can you get a ride home with somebody else? I'm sort of busy right now.'

Jesus! *Already?*

I can almost hear Kirby blushing. 'Heh, heh, thanks, ah, Gwen.' He's giggling nervously.

'Yeah, whatever. I'll just take the broom that was up your ass. Call me tomorrow. Kay?'

I walk away before they answer. Shaz is passed out on the couch. I can't be bothered rousing her. I hitch a ride home with some random guy and give him five bucks for gas. It's only 12.30 but I'm so tired. My message light's blinking when I get in. Oh, God, it's from my friend Jess.

*

Jess is the only person I know who is as, or is even more neurotic than I am. She goes to a great school and is twenty. We met a while ago when I had a shoot at her campus for an Abercrombie ad. She was one of the only models picked from the ACC schools; the rest were booked from New York agencies. She's a trip and a half. Totally unbelievable. We have this ongoing joke about living together one day. Believe me that couldn't happen. We'd end up dead.

Don't get me wrong, Jess is superb, but our neuroses are sort of synonymous. We're both walking disorders. She doesn't have an eating problem per se either. She was only hospitalized because of it about six years ago. Every year since I've met her, at about that time, I send her balloons and a Happy Anniversary card. I would send her a cake, but that's futile, like she'd eat it.

She doesn't wanna model. I respect that. It'd be kind of tough for her to do much more than Juniors' stuff. She's only 5 feet 3 inches and that's too small. So she's set her sights on acting. Actually she's touring the pageant right now. Er, at least she wants to. She was in Miss Virginia – I don't know how that turned out. Hopefully good. Her platform is, ironically enough, self-esteem in children. Funny, since she has none of her own, but it's all good. We like to make light of it.

Anyway, I push the light and the message is as follows:

'Hey, Gwen, it's me Jessica. [Deep breath] Well, I made it!

I'm Miss Virginia. I'm soiling myself as we speak. I'm sorry I didn't tell you sooner but I just got back from an audition for a soap pilot and I just found out and the pageant is three weeks away. Anyway, before I go to Atlantic City I wanna see you and hang out for good luck. OK, sweetie? Gimme a call back and we'll discuss. [Kissing noise] Luv ya, bubbye.'

Well damn! That's so cool for Jess. Aw, I'm so happy, I mean the good things keep pouring in. Shit, it's one. Oh well, she's probably up doing some ridiculous exercise regime, or worrying about something, so I'll call her.

The phone rings.

'Hello?' A perky female voice answers. OK you're not Jess.

'Um, hi, is Jess there please?'

Pause, annoyed silence. 'Yeah. hold on a sec ... JESSICA! Telephone!'

'OK ... I got it.'

'Jess?' I ask, already slightly weary. 'Please don't tell me this conversation will make me need a Xanax.'

'GWEN! Hey, sweetie!'

'Hi! What's up, babe? I got your message, I am so unbelievably stoked!'

'Oh, thanks. I know, I can't believe it myself. I am still coming down.'

'Definitely, I can imagine. How are the harpies handling it?'

'Huh?'

'Who answered the phone?'

'Oh, that was Dana.'

'Why were her panties in a knot?'

'Oh, she's pissed at me for a change.'

'What now?'

'Andrew was totally freaking me out and I sorta spazzed and left the place a mess and they almost threw out all my stuff and I kinda went berserk.'

'God, they're evil. I can't believe you're still with Andrew.'

'I know, but he keeps me grounded. He's my rock.'

'What about the Lord?' I say, sarcastically.

She laughs. 'Nah, he's not really in the picture right now. No, but like everything was in trashbags by the door to my room.'

'Not your clothes?'

'Yup.'

'Fucking-A, that's sacrilege. They must be shot.'

'I agree. I swear one of these days I'm gonna have a breakdown.'

'Aw, don't . . . I've been there and done that, not everyone thinks it's as amusing as we do.'

'True.'

'So what's this I hear about Miss Virginia?'

'I told you . . . I got it, I won!'

'That's just incredible. Honey, we must go out and celebrate.'

'Of course, that's why I called. When can you come down?'

'Whenever. Please, I can't be bothered with school. I'm not even concerned.'

'How about next weekend?'

'Sounds chill to me. I don't have any shoots as of yet, but if I do I'll cancel.'

'Don't go to any trouble or anything.'

'No, I so wanna see you! We'll have a blast.'

'Oh shit, Gwen, one of the harpies needs to call her boyfriend, I've gotta jet.'

'Wahey! All right, I'll drop you an e-mail and let you know for sure. Take care!'

'You too, sweetie. Love ya!'

'Bye.'

'Bye.'

Aw, it's always so good to talk to Jess. I wonder what's up with Andrew. Jesus is he possessive. Andrew's like this on-again-off-again boyfriend of hers. He's almost as psychotic as she is. Like, he goes on these drunken rampages and almost kills himself any time they have a tiff, which occurs almost daily. So you can imagine the stress she encounters. They all make fun of Andrew because sometimes he's effeminate. OK, his name's Andrew Neero but they all call him Queero. Because, seriously, people thought he was homosexual. I mean he's so not. He's a really cool guy, just intense. But he's pretty narcissistic and at times can be really flagrant.

Greg Benjamin

He's a frat boy and therefore drinks like a Kennedy. And he and Jack Daniel's don't mix. There have been several incidents where he has pledged his undying love to Jess and almost severely hurt someone. I will give you just a few choice times.

1. The time he and Jess were having a fight because Jess went to some Formal at another guy's frat. In her defense, the other guy was the friend of the boyfriend of one of her sorority sisters and he needed a date. So, after drinking about five shots of Jagermeister and perhaps half a keg, Andrew proceeded to literally throw himself off Jess's third-story balcony. He was hanging on to a railing and had to be pulled up by campus security.

2. When Jess told him to give her space because she was having personal problems. He later saw her at the library studying with one of her theater friends who wasn't straight anyway. Andrew, already intoxicated at three o'clock in the afternoon, dragged the poor drama fag out of the library and proceeded to beat him with a shoe.

3. During Jess's sorority rush when she didn't have time to hang out with him as much, he began calling her periodically just breathing, not saying

anything. He usually did this after several ounces of Jim Beam, forgetting that Jess had caller ID.

4. The time I visited Jess and read her tarot cards. They said a breakup was imminent and he went sprinting out of the house to clear his head. He was so disturbed by this portent that he collided with a cyclist and broke his leg.

I could go on and on. But I don't want to. Anyway, I'm tired and I need my beauty sleep.

'JUST ANOTHER MANIC MONDAY'
(IN AN ALL TOO LITERAL SENSE)

MONDAY. I HATE THE FUCKING ALARM. AGAIN, IT GOES OFF AT
5.42. Something in my bones tells me it's gonna be a shitty day
outside so at least I don't have to dress too summery. I shower
and do my 650 crunches. I decide to dry my hair stick straight
and tie the front part back in hippie braids with flower clips. I
put on this long, baggy, retro-looking navy, brown and white
Pamela Dennis dress and Mia three-inch brown sandals.

The 'rents are still sleeping so I take a water bottle and my
300 pills and jet. I was right. It's already overcast and humid as
a bitch. Luckily, I had put extra-smoothing wax in my hair
because otherwise it would be frizzing like mad.

I haven't been to school in what seems like weeks. All my
teachers are shocked to see me. I still have A's in the majority
of my classes. I've been keeping up with the work, surprisingly.

Landed

History is boring as shit. But what's to be expected. We watch this dumb movie on the 1930s so while that's running I mentally go over my closets of clothes and determine what still needs to be bought for spring.

In psych, Grendel is happy to see me. Frankly, I don't give a shit. He's still wormy. We're discussing depression. I make a note to myself not to go to his class for the remainder of the week since I know everything there is to know about that subject.

French – who knows? Like I can understand what she says half the time. It doesn't matter she's a sweet woman and, to her credit, can dress well. I think we're doing something with reflexive verbs but I've been to Paris for shows enough times to know the important sayings: 'Stay away from me, dirtbag!' And, 'I'd rather die, Eurotrash!'

Honors chorus – blah. Our teacher is a fat Nazi. He reminds me of Hitler. He doesn't like me because of my deviant religious beliefs ... being pagan. It's all good. He had a problem with my Mexican friend, Mariana, and my bisexual friend, Angel. We're all gonna sew sequined swastikas to our tuxedos for the spring concert. That is if I'm here.

Lunch is uneventful. Surprise, I don't eat. Kirby and Leigh go out to lunch and Shaz goes to her car to call Chris. God, that's all she talks about now. So I go to my car and chat with Tyrone and set up shoots for the following week. DKNY ad

69

campaign in three weeks, and a Jean Paul Gaultier show that's iffy in a month. His last show didn't go over too well so it's still up in the air.

My English teacher isn't there, thank God. But we have Slutstitute. Slutstitute is this vile woman with trailer-trash hair, fake tan and shit figure. She wears white all the time. Not winter white, but trashy-ass-Jordache-jeans white and she always busts out of her clothes. It's repulsive. She looks like an opossum. I kid you not. We have to do some analytical, writing about *Wuthering Heights*, which is easy so I finish in no time and talk to Shaz for the rest of the period.

Trig is hard as shit. I'm so lost, I'm thinking of dropping it. My teacher is fast and the material's hard. Plus, being sixth period, my mid-afternoon tranquilizer starts kicking in and I'm usually asleep. But I have a 78 percent and if I beg I can bring it up.

Our physics teacher isn't in school either, which comes as no surprise. Fine with me, I take off early and head over to the Y. I do a vigorous workout. Luckily, Repulsive Old Man is yet to be seen. Thank God for small favors. Unfortunately, Preteen Slut is. She's almost as hideous. She wears this God-awful burgundy sports bra and Spandex number that only accentuates her white, flabby gut. She doesn't work out properly, my biggest pet peeve, and has an even more repugnant crony with whom she associates. If I had eaten anything today I would throw it up. I leave immediately upon seeing her, having already worked out for two hours.

It's still raining which isn't doing wonders for my hair. Oh well. I call the woman from the beach when I get home and confirm our house. I'm lucky 'cause she had another interested buyer. Tough titties though. Ya snooze, ya lose. Anyway, I just lay low for the rest of the night. Shaz and I talk briefly because she needs to call Chris. And Leigh touches base with me before she goes to Kirby's.

God, everyone has somebody. Boohoo. Yeah, I have my problems. I pop another Xanax.

Mondays suck.

Oh, thrilled to see my alarm is going off at 5.42 pronto once again. Goddamn Panasonic! Today promises to be nicer, says the local weatherman. Bullshit. I can just sense the humidity already. I'm not gonna bother styling my hair. So I shower and since it's Tuesday I have to exfoliate and shave my legs. God bless, with that taken care of I'm almost all set. Do my crunches, blah, blah, blah.

Shit, I wore a dress yesterday so I guess a skirt is not an option. Oh and a PS to all who feel that skorts are a viable alternative. May you rot in hell. I think the designer of skorts should be mauled by cats. I'm sure they are in the same family as the person who invented a spork. Unless your name is Jonboy and you're eating pork and beans out of a can, I think a multi-purpose utensil is utter crap. I mean, I won't even touch my sorbet with a salad fork.

What to wear? Jesus, I'm in a pissy mood. Awesome, I'm getting my rag. Luckily, I don't get pimples. But cramps are another story. I should wear something comfortable to relieve the bloaty feeling. Ugh. Oh, OK, I've got my mineral-colored Nicole Miller drawstring clamdiggers and ecru linen peasant's blouse by Cloud 9. It looks cute. And I can tie my hair in a chignon. Crisis averted. 6.51 and no Xanax yet. The day is starting off slightly positively.

I grab a half a grapefruit since I need to nurse my ovaries. Or whatever the hell it is that causes me this monthly torment. I doubt I will have children. Procreation is not an option, not with the pain it causes. My dad had kidney stones and still winces when we drive on gravel. I can't imagine passing an eight-pound breathing mass. Oh, God.

I was right. It is humid. Like a fucking sauna. For some odd reason this intensifies my cramps. I can't be bothered today. Plus, Tyrone is supposed to call and confirm my appointments for the week. I can't keep checking my car phone every three minutes. And my chronic dehydration spiel is getting a little old. Oh well, I'm taking my phone with me into school. If anyone has a problem they can take it up with Amazon Gwen: Menstrual Maiden!

Landed

History sucks ass. Notes all period. Like I give a shit about FDR. Unless he's a designer, count him off my list. I've got a fourteen-point plan I'd like to employ right about now. I am so pissy. My bad. What's gonna irk me further is that Shaz and Leigh are all post-period and glowing like light bulbs.

Grendel is as queer as usual. I can't stand this little gnome. He called on me to discuss the history of depression and I barked at him and called him a sadistic little troll. My head is obviously down for a reason, cupcake.

Oh, so just as I get finished being Queen Bitch my cellphone starts ringing. I have to start screaming and pretending I'm having a seizure. Grendel almost goes into cardiac arrest and I run to the bathroom to answer my phone.

'Ty?'

'Hey, baby.'

'Who is this?'

'Gwen, it's Riley. Chill, dude.'

'Sorry, man, I'm ragging. I have been a total bitch all day. What's up?'

'Not much, I just wanted to say, hey. Oh, and I also wanted to tell you that Chris is really pissing me off.'

'How so?'

'He's obsessed with that Shaz chick. I mean twentyfour-seven it's this Shaz girl like all the time. I think our plan backfired. He got his first piece of ass and now he's struck.'

'Personally, Ri, I think it's cute. But I know what you mean. Shaz is getting all haughty about it too. Frankly, I'm not concerned. Let her get her's now. She deserves it.'

'Yeah, I guess you're right.'

'Oh, incidentally, why are you calling me at 9.40 on a Tuesday? Shouldn't you be sleeping on some big-breasted model?'

'Nah, she left.' I can almost hear him grinning. 'Actually, I'm in town. Er sorta. I'm in OC, checking on our place. That woman you spoke to, she called me to check it out.'

'Hey, that's awesome. I've gotta come meet you.'

'Hey, yeah!' he goes sarcastically. 'Why'd you think I was calling?'

'The laugh's on you, dumbass. No nookie for you. My aunt's in town.'

'Oh, shit. Forget it then. Just joshing, baby, I just wanted to chill anyway.'

'Cool.' I smile. 'I'm not giving any head either.' Why must I always be so flirtatious.

'Damn, girl, you're killing me.'

My Tuesday's perking up.

FORGED NOTES/FORGED PROMISES

SO I'M STOKED NOW. I JUST FORGE SOME THERAPIST'S NOTE so I don't get pink-slipped. The teachers can be real dicks about that. This stupid bitch who I barely know who volunteers in the office or something wants to know why I'm never here. She's this Indian chick named Nacho or something. I am like, please, as if it's any of your concern.

She's so nosy. She lives through other people. Like supposedly she's friends with these two girls who graduated a year earlier. One's named Karen and the other Laura. They're the only other people at my school I was remotely friends with. They're in New York right now. Both are actresses. Actually, Laura majors in music at Odelphi. Karen was going to NYU but I think she landed some cable soap, so college may be in limbo. Anyway, she followed these girls like a trained dog. I don't think they could stand her.

One time Karen had come over and Nacho, or Neina's her name, she came too. We were playing witch games or whatever. And we were playing ouija board and this spirit came on and wanted to come into the room and talk with us. I dunno, Neina really freaked out. It's not against her religion; she's not even Hindu, she's Baptist. She just chickened out.

Ever since then I can't stand her. She's loud too. So whenever she talks to me I just walk by with my nose up. And I'm curt. I'm sorry, honey, but I've got people to see.

So other than her, no one gives me any shit in the office. And I'm off to OC to see Riley. No, Gwen, do not go pick up condoms. You don't need them . . . remember?

I guess in a way I'm excited to see him. My thing with Riley is weird. Yes, I do have feelings but we both don't take each other seriously. I don't wanna get too attached and I'm sure all Riley wants is some ass. But meanwhile, I kinda talked to Chris about it, I know, I'm stupid, and he said that all Riley does is talk about me. Yeah, that's flattering but it just makes things complicated. I'm so nervous that I'll fall for him that I try to keep a distance. Oh, I know it's not healthy, but when did I claim to be the epitome of well-being?

Riley wants to meet me somewhere nice but not too fancy. That's fine. I'm not demanding Wolfgang Puck or anything. I'm kinda anxious to see him, not that you could tell. I'm shaking more than usual and, yes, I confess I did go home to change. I'm now wearing a skirt. Shut up, I wore a dress yesterday, not a skirt, plus Riley didn't see me. It's cute. It's Cerutti and lavender and really short. And I'm also wearing this pale lavender, yellow and sage Prada shirt. Both are relatively new. And I did have to fix my hair all over again. I always take great pains with my looks, though. I mean, I'm not falling for him. This is the part where you're supposed to help me out. C'mon now.

OC is still relatively dead. It's early spring so I guess that's to be expected. I hate when there's no sun out and it's hazy as a bitch. I put my AC on and blast some Hole. My opinion of Courtney Love has totally changed. I must give her mad props for becoming glam. She looks good now. And her music is kickass.

Shit, I just passed the restaurant where I'm supposed to meet him. I see his car too. Well, at least that's a good thing. I hate being the first one to arrive on dates. Oopsie, total illegal Ueey, but if a cop saw me he'll get over it. OK, good, breathe, you're here. God, Gwen, complete shit parking job. Oh well, no one uses both handicap spots anyway. Here he comes... why am I all nervous? Come on, this is Riley.

He's wearing a three-quarter-length black leather jacket and baggy khakis. Probably all Armani. He's also got an over-sized white dress shirt on and lots of beaded necklaces. And... he's taller than me. FUUCCCKKKK.

He reaches out and gives me a big hug and then a sloppy kiss. I swat him away. He grins and we go inside.

'So, Gwenster, what's been going on?'

We seat ourselves and the busboy brings us water and menus.

'Oh, same old shit, Ri, you know, the norm. How about you? What's been happening in your head?'

'Nothing, baby, just been thinking about you.' He does that two-finger kiss thing and does the perfect imitation of a Backstreet Boy.

'Oh, Riley,' I swoon, 'how'd you know white trash is my weakness?' I smile slowly at him.

He fills me in on what's been happening at Ford and this new Tommy campaign he's doing, which incidentally I'm up for too. Then we get to talking about Shaz and Chris.

'Well, personally, I think it's hysterical,' I say. 'I mean, here Shaz is, horny as a dog in heat, and Chris comes along chafing at the bit to get some and they get along great. Especially since he's so docile. Shaz is a total control freak. I bet she brings out the beast in him. I know she's gotta have a whole set of whips and chains hidden somewhere. I bet they've already used them.'

Riley's eyes flash. 'Nah. I think they're totally into role playing. Chris left his wallet out and there was a receipt next to it for cop and schoolgirl costumes. I know there isn't any theme party they're attending.'

'Oh, God, this is so sick. I can't believe we're sitting here discussing our best friends' sex life.'

He turns serious. 'Well then, let's talk about ours.'

Huh? 'Riley, what do you mean?'

'Come off it, Gwen. I'm crazy about you. And I think you have feelings for me. I know everything's been all casual and haphazard in the past but I think we should experiment a little. I wanna get to know the real you.'

'No you don't.' Could he be serious? I don't have intimacy issues but when he sees the real me, the funny, nutty, quirky Gwen is just gonna seem like a psycho.

'Gwen, at least think about it. I really like you.' He pauses and gives me this quizzical smile. He means it. I can tell. ARGGH! Why does this always happen? 'I have a surprise for you,' he says. He flashes a key.

'Is that to our summer house?'

'Yup.'

'Well,' I sigh. 'You know what that means. Forget lunch, we've got an apartment to christen.'

He jumps up. 'All right!' He starts walking away. 'Wait a minute. I don't want you thinking this is all some ploy to have sex. I do really care about you.'

'I know.' I smile sarcastically. 'That's what scares me. The sex is to take my mind off it.'

He puts his arm around me and has no idea how serious

I'm being. Damn! It looks like I'll have to stop at the drugstore after all.

For a while it's getting pretty hot and heavy, and then I remember I'm surfing the crimson. Riley's disappointed but he'll live. I whack him off so he doesn't get blue balls.

The place is really nice inside. And with a good decorator it'll be even nicer. We're all so stoked about living there. It's gonna be incredibly phat. It's almost three. I've gotta go work out and then I'm off to play volleyball. I give Riley a hug and another session almost starts up again so I leave and he tells me he'll call me soon.

On the way home I just start crying uncontrollably. I have no idea why. This happens to me sometimes. I think it's all the pent-up emotion I keep inside. Either that or medicinal build-up. Either or. So I'm cruising down Route 50 with tears streaming down my face. It's awful.

I work out for an hour. I don't do cardio because I'm gonna play volleyball at the college. There's a beach court out there and on sunny days it's a good way for me to tan and get some exercise. The usual people are out there. And I play fairly well considering I'm the only chick out there. Plus, I've even got height on some of them. I hate short people.

The guys don't go easy on me either. But I hate it when they get all patronizing or try to pretend they're playing lightly. I can handle their shit. So I just trash talk right back to them. Some of them are afraid to cuss in front of me. I don't care. I'll say fuck in front of the best of them. It's not like I give a shit.

I play really well today. I stay on for three games with a friend of mine and then I realize I have to go because I have therapy at seven. My therapist is cool. I really don't go to him to talk. We just shoot the shit and he checks up on my meds. Today's no different. I'm already in a pissy mood because I've been waiting while he's been talking to this socially phobic truckdriver. He tries to be friendly but I'm in a bitchy mood. I think he gets the picture. He asks how things are going and then writes me a few more refills for Xanax. God bless him.

I realize on my way home I haven't eaten anything for a few days, so I stop by the Giant and pick up some couscous. My parents are taking the dog for a walk. So I call Shaz and catch up on my homework. Shaz is talking blah, blah, blah, about Chris. And I think she gets mad because I'm really bitchy to her. But you know I'm not concerned. I mean I just can't deal today.

I talk to Leigh and she's really sympathetic. Which I can so count on her to be. She listens and offers some good advice but is meeting Kirby at the movies in fifteen minutes so has to go. Once again I'm alone. Oh well. Three more days till I go down to see Jess. I really need a break.

*

Leigh is actually happy when I tell her about Riley. For some odd reason she thinks I need somebody. Why doesn't anybody get me? I have no idea but it sure pisses me off. Anyway, I'm glad I got to see Riley. It definitely beat school and it'll be excused 'cause I have a whole drawer full of doctor's excuses.

I'm feeling kinda shaky though. More so than usual. It's not because I didn't get any either. I hate feeling happy. It scares me. Plus I'm worried that I'm gonna fall for somebody. Maybe if I call Shaz again it'll alleviate my fears.

I pick up the phone and dial her number.

'Hello.'

'Shaz, it's Gwen.'

'What's up?'

'Listen, I need to talk to you.'

'OK...about?'

'I just saw Riley.'

'For real? Is Chris with him?'

'No, dumbass, but thanks for your concern. I just hooked up with him.'

'How, aren't you ragging?'

'Well, I mean, I didn't get some if you catch my drift.'

'Drift caught. Is that why you're antsy...because you didn't get your turn?'

'No, I mean...no! Riley told me that he really cares for me and I am unsure of my feelings.'

'That's good...right? I mean, yes, Gwen, we do want people to like us.'

Yeah, at least she does. She likes that a little too much.

'I know, Shaz, but it's not the same thing. It's not something I'm happy about. I feel like I'm living up to some expectation. Riley knows me but he doesn't. Our relationship is really just surface with sex thrown in for shits and giggles. He doesn't know the real me... I'm just afraid that if he does, he'll wish he hadn't.'

'Please, Gwen. Stop being so fucking cynical. You're so masochistic it's retarded. You've gotta learn to give people a chance. I didn't think I'd ever find a guy who'd live up to my expectations, and now that I have... I couldn't be happier.'

Being on the rag, I didn't need to hear any of this. 'Whatever, Shaz. You're just happy now that you're finally getting some. I can't talk to you about this now, I gotta go.'

I hang up the phone. She's too lovestruck or whatever right now to be upset with me. I, frankly, am not concerned. I debate calling Jess but I decide against it. She's got play practice all this week and won't be home till late. It's weird. Normally, I would consult the tarot, but intuitively I feel today is not the best of times. Besides, I feel lazy as shit. I decide to take a bath instead.

Even with aromatherapy and two glasses of chardonnay I still feel shitty. It's getting late and I better go to bed. I pop like two or three Seconals and climb into bed where I am welcomed by a blanket of white, luscious sleep.

Awesome. My alarm doesn't go off until 6.12 for some odd reason. Actually I think I just slept through it. Those pills knock you out. This means that I have to haul ass to get ready. Granted it doesn't take me that long to shower and do crunches but please bear in mind all the obsessive compulsive rituals I must complete before I feel ready to take on the day.

Today I decide on a muted beige embroidered shirt jacket and capris by Miu Miu and I put my hair up in hairsticks. At least I don't have to worry about drying it. I can tell I'm starting to lose more weight which is a good thing so I grab a water and my pills and head out the door. The sun is shining and it's kinda cool with a slight breeze in the air. I still keep my windows down with the AC on since I have this thing about foreign air.

No sooner do I step out of my car than my cellphone goes off. I'm shocked. In fact, I almost shit. I hope it's not Riley because after yesterday I couldn't handle anything else. But if I remember right he went to Baltimore to stay with some of his friends who go to Loyola, so I should be safe. Besides, it's about eight in the morning. It's way too early for him to be getting up and a little too late for him to be rolling back in.

My fears are allayed . . . it's Ty.

Landed

'Hey, sugar, what's up?'

'Ty, baby,' I say, surprised. 'What's going on?'

'Girl, you don't even need to know why I'm up this early but I have some news for you. You landed that Tommy campaign. It's being shot on location next Thursday in West Hollywood. You're going to LA!'

'Awesome. Good, that's like the one campaign I really wanted. Is it binding though? Can I do work for anybody else for the time being?'

'Yeah, that's the good thing. They're being pretty laid back and they don't wanna sign with you exclusively. I'm happy. I'm getting my 10 percent.'

'Mmm, go on, boy. Now you can buy yourself some real Armani.'

'Uh? Oh girl, don't get me started. Now I've gotta go. I'm Fedexing two plane tickets to you. They should arrive by the weekend. Cool?'

'Cool. Ciao, Ty.'

'Smooches.'

The phone clicks. What a camp. Well, at least my day is starting out better. Praise Allah.

The rest of the day flies by. I get to talk with Leigh some 'cause Kirby's not here today and she gives me some further advice on the whole Riley deal. She doesn't think I should sweat it, just give it a chance. She hasn't talked to Shaz but doesn't think she's mad at me. We both know she's way too hung up on Chris. I'm glad I get to talk to her. It's not that I'm jealous of her relationship with Kirby, I just wanna have my friend back.

I work out again but the weather turns to shit so I can't play volleyball outside. It's all good. I just do extra cardio. My workout feels good today, for a change, and I feel less burnt out. I'm proud of myself, only one Xanax today. Yay. And no self-destructive thoughts . . . er, as of yet. Anyway, I call Jess when I get home and confirm things for the weekend. Two days early and my stuff's already packed. By the time the day comes to leave, I'm ready.

Watch out, Bellevue, here we come.

SOUTHERN BELLE(VUE)

TODAY I SPARE MYSELF. NO, I DON'T GET UP AT THE USUAL 5.42, which is a nice reprieve. Instead, the birds are chirping and it's 7.36 before I climb out of bed. The sun's already shining and I can tell it's gonna be a great day. I know, greatness... scary, isn't it? I shower and blow-dry my hair straight. Shave my legs, exfoliate... gotta look good. I need traveling clothes though, something casual but flirty. I decide on white clamdiggers by DKNY and a rich pink sweater by BCBG. I look refreshed and ready to go.

I only have about fourteen outfits packed. Stuff for all occasions. There's no telling what kinda mess Jess and I will get into. Last time at her boyfriend's fraternity Halloween mixer we made a ruckus. We went to this restaurant fifteen minutes away from grounds. We were all dressed in costume and most of us had been pregaming before hand. Jess and I were both dressed up as 1980s film stars; don't even ask. So there we were just chilling in this upstairs room of the restaurant all to ourselves. The waitress was really cool. She went to Virginia too. She didn't even ask us for IDs. We were set. Andrew's friends kept buying us rounds and rounds of shots and, of course, we couldn't refuse. And after about our eighth shot we got a little rowdy.

Jess and I thought it would be hilarious if we went downstairs pretending to actually be the film stars. We started accosting all these old couples and like screaming at them because we were past our prime. The restaurant manager thought it was kinda funny but we still had to be escorted back upstairs by two of the busboys.

Anyway, I get outta here pretty early. The drive to Virginia isn't that bad. I have to go around Washington and on the Beltway. But it's fine once I get on Route 29.

The Beltway traffic is always a bitch though. Only everyone has road rage, including yours truly. I just can't be bothered with people who don't go at least 20 m.p.h. over the speed limit. I zigzag out of the lanes and I sorta pass someone illegally off of one of the exits. Don't look so shocked! Everyone's fine . . . it's all good. Meanwhile, this Hispanic man in this nasty pre-1976 lowrider truck keeps staring at me and following me as I weave between the lanes. He's obviously trying to talk to me. Please, I will have no part of this. Jesus God! OK, fine. I roll down my window and am like yelling because we're only going about 85 m.p.h. and there's no traffic lights anywhere to stop.

'Hey, baby!' he says, with this hideous accent. My God, I'm gonna be sick.

'Yeah, um, hi...look is there something you wanted... because you've been following me around for twenty minutes?'

He points to his friend, who I didn't notice earlier. He's even greasier and more repulsive than this guy. I can practically smell them even through all the wind resistance. His friend half stands up in his seat.

'I got something for you, senorita!' He pulls down his pants. And they wonder why that Mexican food had hepatitis!

This only happens to me like thirty-two times a day in New York, so I'm used to it. I flip him off and mutter something obscene and then race ahead.

The rest of the drive is calm. Once I get off the Beltway it's fairly easy. It's so pretty with the mountains off on either side of the highway and flowers blooming and cows everywhere. It's so pastoral it makes me sick. I have to pee so bad but of course I'm not gonna stop. I have this tremendous phobia of public restrooms. I drive straight to my hotel. I'm probably gonna stay the night at Jess's but I wanna have a hotel room just in case. Plus, I cannot live without my own shower.

I check in. Everything's cool. It's about three o'clock. I'm sure Jess is still in class. The bed looks really comfortable and I'm ass tired. So maybe I'll take a little nap. And for once, without the aid of sleeping pills, I drift off into dreamland.

Fuck it! It's 6.30. Jess must be worried sick. I call her place and she answers.

'Hello.'

'Hey, Jess, honey, it's Gwen.'

'Gwen, oh man, where are you? I've been worried sick!'

'Sorry, I got to my hotel room three hours ago and I fell asleep.'

'Don't worry about it. So when can you be over here?'

'Well, I gotta shower...'

'Dammit! So what, I'll expect you tomorrow?'

'Heh, heh. No, I'll be over in like an hour. What should I wear, what's going on tonight?'

'Well, I thought we'd eat a big dinner.' She laughs wryly. 'No, seriously, we're just gonna drink over here for a little bit and then head over to my friend Scott's frat. They're having some huge party with a band.'

Awesome. Agoraphobia! 'Cool, so night clothes appropriate for going out and getting trashed?'

'Sounds peachy.'

'Grand, I will see you in a little.'

'God bless.'

Landed

'Bye.'

'Bye.'

Oh man. I love partying but sometimes these huge ones where I only know two people make me paranoid. Oh, well. I pop a few Xanax for good measure.

The shower's actually not bad. The water pressure's decent and I get a really good shampoo. I condition my hair and put in a mask and then dry off. I decide on an in-between length skirt by Chloe and a midriff Versace shirt. It's fairly simple. It's almost got cap sleeves and it's very tight. The neck is this square boatneck that shows off my collar bone. I dry my hair straight and slick it back. My makeup's on and I'm set. Uh oh. Here we go.

Jess's apartment isn't exactly a sty. But, realistically, it's not exactly the Hilton either. She shares it with four other girls, all of whom are much neater than she. Her relationships vacillate. Jess isn't a hard person to get along with. Well, at least in my opinion, so I guess maybe you need some serious psychoses to understand her. Her room-mate is this girl from Philadelphia who is nice enough but on occasion borders on mega bitch. She has this obsession with toilet paper, as odd as it is. You know like some people fill up their gas tank when it's three-quarters full. This girl, Dana, is like that with toilet paper. I almost bought stock in Charmin' after seeing their bathroom. It's insane.

Jess's friends border on abnormal. She has two sets. One is the mainstream, jock–frat and pretty–smart crowd, and the other is the theater bunch. Please, don't get all self-righteous and say that theater people can be normal and pretty or smart or athletic. I'm talking here about the freak theater types. The oddballs, drama fags, prima donnas and heretics that we've all come to associate with drama majors. Some of them, and I'm sorry, Jess, are pure freak.

When I walk in Jess is chilling in the main room with this guy named Freedom and two girls, Persephone and Asia. They're all dressed fairly acceptably. Freedom's about 6 feet 2 inches with dark spiky hair and multiple piercing. He's wearing baggy jeans with paint stains that, had they been intentional, could have passed for Dolce & Gabbana and a white T-shirt probably like Dickey or something and a black leather jacket. Asia is wearing serious bell-bottoms of a pea-green persuasion, and a navy three-quarter-length V-neck shirt that clings to her enormous breasts. She too has dark hair and it's parted and in two braids which reach her shoulders. Persephone is obviously trying to match her namesake and is wearing some cream organza hippie dress and has her long straw-colored hair half up and half down. She's kinda short but really pretty in a very earthy way. They're all sitting around taking bong hits.

'What's up, guys?' I say, as I walk in. The door was open so I felt no need to knock.

Landed

Jess runs up to me squealing and gives me a big hug. She's wearing a black jacket, probably DKNY, and bootcut jeans. She's got a French blue fitted shirt on that I believe is Bebe. I hope I'm not slipping. She then makes the rounds of reintroducing me.

'Gwen, you remember everyone from last time? You guys, do you remember Gwen?'

They all smile sheepishly and shake their heads. No, they don't remember me. I'm not surprised. I saw them about three months ago, briefly. They were all high off their ass anyway.

Freedom comes forward and gives me a high five. 'Hey, man, how's it going?' I smile and do a cool handshake that Riley taught me and then Asia stands up.

'Hi, Gwen, nice to remeet you.' She's got a pleasant voice. Very mellow but mature. It seems to possess this innate knowledge, probably from all the weed she's been smoking. I smile and shake her hand and return her greeting.

Persephone stands up and looks into my eyes. 'How are you, child of God? Wow, you have a very tired soul.'

'That's probably 'cause I just woke up an hour ago. But it's great to meet you.' She wanly returns to her chair.

Jess invites me to sit down and soon we're all chatting like we've been good friends forever. I do about five bong hits and feel a lot more relaxed. It's nearing eight so Jess says we have to go. Asia and Persephone have dance rehearsal and Freedom is

93

actually the singer for the band who's playing at Scott's fraternity. He's gotta hurry up and go ahead so we take my car.

'Damn, this is a phat ride,' he says, as he climbs in the backseat.

'Thanks, man.' I hate myself when I'm high. Every other word to a guy is either man or dude.

Jess immediately starts rambling about Andrew's latest deed. Evidently the other day during one of their off periods, he came running to her house demanding to see her. When she refused, he got all pissy, got really drunk and brought some ho over from Phi Mu and began making out with her right under Jess's window. Now I know Jess is not one to be reckoned with and she fucking hates this Phi Mu bitch anyway because they were in the same pledge class or something so she opens her window and starts throwing things at them. Not like soft stuff either. She's throwing bio books and snowdomes and even a fucking AM–FM radio. Phi Mu ran away but she hit Andrew on his leg with the radio and now he's got a bruise the size of a kumquat on his right calf. I dunno, supposedly they're back together now.

The party's already in full swing when we get there. Freedom kisses each of us before he gets out, an odd sentiment in my opinion, and then races to go set up. Jess and I get out and head inside and we are by far the best-looking ones here. I don't understand sorority girls. Granted, some of them are pretty and can dress, but the majority are American Eagle clones with these rayon floral-print skirts and tanks. It's all I can do not to throw up. And there's the JAP element. The girls with the big brown-and-copper-streaked hair and brown lipstick. They wear black pantsuits everywhere – Jil Sander – but still, they practically scream Long Island. The demure southern ones are cool. And then there's the eclectic mix from everywhere.

The guys are all pretty much standard. Preppy, jock frat wear. Abercrombie, some Tommy, Ralph Lauren and Nautica. Brooks Brothers for the golfers in the crowd. Nobody too chic.

Right now the band's still setting up, so they're playing a lot of 1980s music and Jess and I are dancing. We're both fucked up beyond belief and pretty soon a bunch of rowdy-looking frat guys without shirts start dancing really nastily beside us. It gets kind of gross.

After the song I try to walk away, as does Jess, but these fucking penises with ears have us cornered. They're all like, 'Hey, baby, where have you been hiding?'

So I go, 'Obviously not in a good enough place. How about we try it again and you go try to find us?'

The one guy says, 'Heh, heh, really funny. I wonder if you're that feisty in bed.'

And I say, 'Probably more feisty than your right hand, asswipe, but you'll never find that out.'

All the guys are drunk and are like, Oooh, making that cold bust noise. Random shirtless frat guy is getting really pissed. All of a sudden the tallest of the three reaches out and grabs Jess's boob. I go off. I drop my purse and punch the fucker square in his jaw. Jess then screams and knees him in his nutsack. It grows dead quiet.

Out of nowhere, Andrew comes charging with this banshee-like wail and tackles all three guys. Oh, God, I'm thinking, not a brawl. So some of their boys and some of Andrew's boys all jump in and pretty soon it's like WWF. Jess and I are too dumbstruck to do anything. Campus police can't be called since we're off grounds. Finally, some members of another frat break them all up. Jess and I go sit down on a couch in a back room while everything calms down.

'Are you OK?' I ask her, smiling.

She just starts cracking up and we both just fall over laughing.

'I don't even know what's so funny!' she says, in between breaths.

'I don't either...I've taken my medicine today!'

'Me too.'

We laugh a few minutes longer and tears are falling down our faces. My mascara's running like Flo Jo. We both get up, still completely trashed, and stumble back into the main room. Freedom's band is already playing. They're really good.

Landed

Someone had said they were ska...and I was like, oh, Jesus, but luckily they're modern rock with some classic stuff thrown in.

Andrew comes to see us a little later. He's got a cut on his chin and a black eye. Jess and I bust out laughing when we see him. He's grinning kinda sheepishly but he appears like he's really upset. He and Jess go off into some room upstairs, probably to fuck, and I chill on one of the downstairs couches. By the time they return it's about two. I need to sleep in a real bed. So Andrew takes me back to the hotel. I thank him and tell Jess I'll see her tomorrow. I need to remember to wash my face.

HANGOVERS, LAYOVERS, FUCKOVERS

I DON'T KNOW WHAT WAS IN THAT WEED WE HAD LAST night. Technically, I shouldn't say what was *in* that weed, I should say what kind of weed was it. I bet it was laced with something hardcore. Actually, the three Xanax I consumed beforehand could not have helped. Anyway, it's like 9.45. I feel worse than buttcrack. My God. Miraculously, when I got back to the hotel room I had the sense to wash my face, rehang my clothes and get changed for bed. I guess that's one of the advantages of being obsessive compulsive. I doubt Jess is even up yet.

Before getting ready, I head down to the gym in (cringe) Spandex shorts and sports bra. I do 1,500 crunches, my leg workout and twenty minutes of cardio. I never let up.

I decide to take a shower and a long one at that. I don't have to deep-condition my hair this morning which is a plus, so I

Landed

just stand in the hot water for about twenty minutes. I put a smoothing serum and some power gel in my hair, brush it out and let it air-dry curly.

It's about 75 degrees out, or at least it's gonna be, plus it's slightly breezy. Being April, I think it's somewhat of a faux pas to wear shorts since it's spring clothes and not yet summer. But that's my opinion. I put on a black backless shirt I got at Episode and a pair of cropped trousers by Laundry. By the time I've gotten ready and taken my 300 pills it's after twelve.

I give Jess a ring but she's already left. Well, damn. What to do, what to do? Charlottesville has shit shops so I can't really buy terribly much. The guys' volleyball club team has a match at twelve so I think I'll go watch that.

By the time I get to Slaughter, the gym where they play, the match has already started. The curator, for lack of a better job description, of this gym is this enormous man with sweatshorts and a Virginia rugby shirt on. He's got his bitch with him, an anemic looking skank with long, limp, mousy-brown hair and fucked-up teeth. They give me a hard time about not having ID. I have to explain to them that I'm visiting and wanna check out the volleyball game since this is one of my prospective college choices. Yeah, right. They're hesitant because they think I'm in my twenties but I show them my real driver's license and they let me in.

Virginia's playing NC State and they're playing like crap.

I mean, I could do better and this is a guys' team. They end up losing in three games. During the between-game breaks, I pepper with one of the middle hitters and he's amazed. He asks me if I play for the school here and I reply, no, I don't even live in this state. He asks for my number but I decline. He looks crestfallen. But what can I say... another one bites the dust.

I really don't feel like sitting in this hotass gym, wrinkling my Episode, epsecially since after its recent closing, it'll be a collector's item. I leave after NC State plays Clemson, the other team in the trimatch. Now what time is it? Shit, my pager is out of batteries. I dunno. Judging by the sun it's like 4.20. Sike, that would only gimme an excuse to smoke a blunt. I pass some random wahoo and ask the time. It's 4.16. Well, damn! Aren't I close? I go to a pay phone and try Jess again. This time she's home.

'Hi, is Jess there please?'

'This is Jessica.'

'Stupid cow, where were you all day?'

'Oh, hey, Gwen. Sorry girl, I forgot I had some audition today for this acting thing over on grounds at eleven. How'd you make out last night?'

'You were there, dumbass. Remember? Andrew took me back to the hotel at around two.'

'Oh yeah, oh yeah. My bad. Sorry, I can't remember shit.

Smoke doesn't usually do that to me.'

'Ohmigod! Same here. It must have been some pretty strong stuff. So, listen, what's the gameplan for tonight?'

'Believe it or not, absolutely jack shit is happening. There are like no parties on Rugby Road.'

'Shut up!'

'I'm totally serious. I guess with exams coming up, people just need to study. Plus, there were tons going on *hier*.'

'True. So whatdya wanna do?'

'Did you bring your witch supplies?'

'A.k.a. my tarot cards and ouija board. Yup. I even brought my candles, but remember what happened last time we tried to do that spell on Andrew?'

'Yeah.' She laughs. 'You know that patch of hair never grew back.'

I bust out laughing. 'So what does that mean? Obviously, we're doing a seance or witch games. What time do you wanna get together?'

'We should probably eat dinner.'

'I should probably not take so many tranquilizers.'

'I'm serious, Gwen. How much have you had to eat today?'

'Um, like at least 800 calories of spring water.'

'You joke now, but you're gonna get sick.'

'Hold on, I have another call. Oh, it's the pot, he's calling the kettle black.'

'Fuck you.' I can hear her smiling, if that's possible. 'I'm trying too, Gwen.'

'Fine, Jesus Christ. Where do you wanna go to dinner? Or do you just wanna go to the hospital and be fed intravenously?'

'Hah, hah. Besides I have a glucose phobia. Let's go to the Biltmore and meet there around seven. That way we can still catch happy hour.'

'Please, I'm gonna have people buying my drinks at regular price.'

'You're a trip. Is that cool?'

'Yeah, it's fine. I'll see you there then.'

'All right, sweetie.'

'Kay, see ya.'

'Bye.'

The phone clicks. Jess is right although I hate to say it. I should probably be eating more. But whatchya gonna do? Anyway, I'm all sweaty. I think I'll head back to the hotel and take a whirlpool. God bless.

Hotel Jacuzzis suck my ass! I swear there are virtually no bubbles and the water is almost tepid. I feel like a goddamn matzah ball or something. On to the showers. I'm not gonna wash my hair again for fear of drying it out, but I do shower off. I'm perplexed as to what to wear. Since it's happy hour I think I should spread my happiness and wear a short skirt. But then again I wore one last night. Oh well, I'll just do a completely different look. And if you even thought I would wear skorts you should be shot!

I put on this short, lilac colored, bateau neck dress designed especially for me by Michael Kors of Celine. I put these silver clips in my hair and I must say I look pretty good. I spray on extra perfume (Greenjeans by Versace, of course) and head on out. And not a moment too soon. I need a margarita!

It's so hard to find parking near the Biltmore since it's up along this side street. There's a mini lot and onstreet parking, but there's never enough spaces. I am pissed because wherever I go I can usually get valet, but I take a deep breath and count this as a learning experience. Luckily, some car is getting out as I circle the lot so I race and grab their spot. Another incoming car glares at me but I'm not concerned at all. Life's a bitch and then you die. That's my mantra.

I sure hope Jess is already here. It's packed. I'm positive there's at least a forty-five-minute wait and, frankly, I don't feel like standing in line sweating next to a bunch of underage frat guys. I see Jess waving from the wooden table she's obviously secured, so once again my fears are allayed.

Jess is with Andrew and his room-mate, Adam. She looks really cute. She's wearing a burgundy shimmery nylon shirt and this tight dark floral-patterned skirt. I think both are by Caché. Andrew's well dressed too. He's got on this light-blue silk and linen polo and a pair of cargo khakis, maybe by True Grit, I think. Adam's just wearing a UVA sweatshirt and jeans. Oh well, not all of us can be couture.

They've all obviously been drinking. A waitress comes by and I order a jumbo margarita and an extra shot of tequila. I must catch up. Andrew smiles at me. 'You remember Adam?'

'Yeah. Hey how are ya?'

Adam laughs and shakes my hand. He's a cool guy. You'd think being pre-med they'd be math-science dorks, constantly absorbed in their calculators. But they're so not like that. Adam plays club soccer. He was offered a varsity position but declined so he could have a life on campus. Novel idea if you ask me.

Anyway, the waitress comes back with my drinks. I do the shot and then start sipping my margarita. The waitress wants to know if we're ready to order. I shake my head but Jess gives me a weary look so I consent. Andrew orders a burger, Adam gets fried quesadillas, and Jess and I get salads. She orders a chicken caesar and I pick a tropical garden. The waitress smiles and takes our menus.

'Well,' I breathe, 'at least that's over and done with.'

For the remainder of the evening we keep drinking and shooting the shit. I pick at my dinner and Jess doesn't even try to bother with me. I am in a generous mood so I pay for dinner, a first for me and then we decide to go back to the guys'

Landed

house to play witch games.

Jess has this obsession with the paranormal. It's fun. I always read her tarot cards when she comes and she takes the reading to heart like it's the gospel. I respect the attention. Hey, if I'm not in control of my life at least I should be in control of someone else's.

There are a bunch of fratties at the house when we get there. Andrew and Adam's fraternity is one of the decent ones on campus. The guys aren't total jerk-offs who make cat calls and consume large quantities of beer and head-butt twenty-fourseven. Yeah, they drink a lot but they also get their work done, which is an admirable trait. They're all pretty friendly when we get there. I don't think I've actually met any of the other guys formally. I've been down to Virginia about five times and the only times I've seen them has been in passing. Most of them are engrossed in the giant TV downstairs so I assume we'll exchange salutations later.

Adam and Andrew's room is miraculously neat. Neat enough to satisfy my neurotic tendencies. They spread out a blanket on the floor and I take my cards and candles out of my purse. See, that's why I love these new Prada strap-on bags. There was a lot of controversy in the fashion industry when they first came out because of their unfortunate resemblance to the fanny pack, but surely smart people must realize that Miuccia Prada wouldn't create something that hideous. Give the woman some credit.

Jess wants me to read her first so she makes the guys leave the room. Adam's fine with this and goes downstairs to get a beer. Andrew's really upset though. He always gets this way. He begs and pleads for her to let him stay and listen in. I try to interject and say that it will mess up the vibes if he crowds her aura, but he won't listen. Jess finally convinces him to go but not without him shooting me some sidelong glance. He's obviously trying to telepathically say not to put any ideas in her head. I dismiss his gaze.

'OK,' I say, once he's left the room, 'how do you wanna do this up?'

'All right, I was thinking of doing it about my general future. Andrew always asks about love questions so I'm sick of him asking me how our relationship is going to turn out. I just wanna find out how I stand in the future.'

'Cool. If he comes up, he does. If he doesn't, no biggie.'

I start to shuffle the cards in the obsessive way I always do, silently chanting to myself. I'm in deep concentration. After about four minutes of shuffling I deal. Uh oh. The layout is in the formation of a Celtic cross. It goes significator, present situation, what crosses, what's beneath, what's behind, what crowns, what's in store for the immediate future, personality, how others perceive you, hopes and fears and, then, final outcome. Jess's life doesn't look too good.

Landed

Everything in the present is in this build-up pattern. She has eight of pentacles reversed, which means craftsmanship. So, basically, it's saying that everything she's worked for is about to be destroyed. She's also got nine of swords and three of swords, defeat and nightmare. The other cards are normal. They've come up before. They just describe what's going on with her and Andrew and with her family life.

I explain all this to Jess and she laughs. She says she knows she's headed for a breakdown and this just confirms it. I give her a hug and we talk for a while and, all of a sudden, Andrew walks in. He wants a reading too but I'm drained. Jess isn't exactly in a spiritual mood anymore, plus Andrew pussies out on some of the other witchy things we do. Like one time, we contacted this spirit named Sara and she started moving things around in the air and shit. No lie! Well, Andrew just went berserk. He tore out of the room as soon as the first dish started floating. Me and Jess were really cool though. We both accepted it like it was normal and kind of got in sync with the spirit. That was the absolute best. Afterwards, Andrew was outside shaking and smoking a few hundred cigarettes to calm his nerves. I dunno what gets into him.

With the witch games out of the way, we're at a loss for things to do. I'm feeling spacy from all the drinks and feel like I'm gonna pass out in a minute. Andrew gets mad at Jess since he can't have a tarot reading and that launches them into another one of their fights. Of course, by this time Andrew's drunk, which doesn't make it conducive to talking things out. He is just yelling and screaming and then starts going off about some guy named Billy who Jess supposedly hooked up with. Jess picks up a magic eight ball and hurls it at Andrew but narrowly misses. I take this as my cue to leave. I give Jess a hug and tell her to be at the hotel at eight tomorrow morning because I have to be on my way early and I wanna get breakfast with her before I go. She hugs me and Andrew stops his ranting to say goodbye. Adam's nice enough to drive me back to the restaurant to get my car, so I don't have to whore myself out for a ride. Thank God.

I get back to my room and there's no messages as of yet so I wash my face and get into bed. I can't sleep and I'm all out of Seconals. Dammit! Oh well, I could try counting sheep. Nah, I am not really too fond of wool. I'll try counting flax plants instead . . .

I glance at my clock and it's 6.50. Shit! I need to get ready if Jess is gonna be here in an hour. Swiftly, I do my 650 crunches and turn on the shower. Since I'm gonna be driving all day I don't take the time to put in any masks, however I do make sure I deep-condition; you should always look your best. I towel dry my hair and put in some texture cream to make sure it dries wavy but not frizzy. I settle on an outfit from Club Monaco: pale peach, cropped long-sleeve shirt and flare chinos.

Landed

Surprisingly, my hair is almost dry as Jess rings the bell.

She's got on a Free People drawstring sweater in yellow and a pair of rinse-colored denim straight-leg jeans. She looks good. We take separate cars and arrive at this bakery on Route 29. Jess and I sit down and both order vegan muffins and water. I eat about one half of mine and Jess only eats a third of hers. She's got a really bad hangover I can tell and I'm sure she was up fighting with Andrew all night. She'll give me the details later. We don't really talk since neither of us is up to it. We sit in this contemplative silence, not saying anything, but projecting meaning. It's something only close friends a lot alike can do. When I've drunk all my water I get up and give Jess a hug and head out on my way. All of a sudden I'm feeling really sad and it's not because I'm saying goodbye. Nor is it because I have a four-hour drive ahead of me because I will go 80 m.p.h. the entire time. Something feels missing. Then I remember Riley's proposition.

I get home in the middle of the afternoon. There's crazy messages on my machine. One's from Ty reminding me of my flight to LA on Tuesday. Hi, of course I remember, I do have a Rolodex. Two are from Shaz, who's all worried about our friendship. One's from Leigh just calling to say hi, and one's from my English teacher.

I can't believe she'd have the gall to call me at home. Her

message says, 'Hi Gwen, this is Ms. Fielding just calling to check up on you. I haven't seen you for a while and I was wondering if you were getting all the work. I'm a little concerned about your participation points. If you're not in school I can't exactly give them to you. Well, since you're out, hopefully you'll get this message and I'll see you in school tomorrow. Bubbye.'

That vegan muffin is gonna come back up with a vengeance! I don't understand why this woman with steel wool for hair is calling me to butt into my life. I simply cannot fathom it. And it burns my bloody ass. On that note, and no pun intended, no, I'm not still ragging. It just gets to me. I have an A in the woman's class but I guess that's not enough. Well, my God, what else does she want? Come on.

I decided to call Shaz back and she is home. We have a heart to heart about our friendship. She realizes that she has been a bit taken with Chris as of late but, still, I was wrong to go off like that. Hey, I can apologize. Anyway, things are all smoothed over between us.

I am very excited about going with Leigh to LA. We should have a blast. Leigh has never accompanied me on any of my shoots before. Plus, LA, aside from all the gangs and assholes, is a really fun place. It actually took a lot of convincing to get Leigh to agree to come. Can you believe that? She is very involved with schoolwork right now. I don't understand. She's got good grades and she's already been accepted into Georgia Tech and that was her first choice. In fact, I'm the only one of my friends not going to college next year. I'm undecided but I think I'm moving out to LA. Shaz is going to Brown, I told you she was a genius. But it's not as if I couldn't go if I did want to. I have the grades and the scores to get in. Plus colleges love having celebrities, ask Claire Danes. It's just that at the point where I am in my life right now, college just doesn't seem like the best solution. I'm making loads of money right now and no one knows how short-lived a model's career can be. Plus, college demands the attention I know I wouldn't be able to give. My parents were kind of upset when I initially decided this. They were all like, what a waste of good brain power. Granted, I got a 1490 on my SATs and a 34 composite on my ACTs. I aced the verbal. You're surprised, huh? I guess 'cause I'm not speaking too pedantically. It's all good though. I mean, this is a decision that I made. And it's the right one...right? Shit, I dunno anymore. Sometimes, I have no idea what I'm thinking.

I have string beans and a protein shake for dinner. I need to stop loading up on carbs. That's like the biggest dieting misconception. That you can eat whatever low fat and still stock up on carbs...No, no. Can't be done. Goes straight to the ass. Many at my school can testify to this case.

I read a little bit but I can't keep my eyes open. That drive really wore me out. I'm butt tired. I get ready and head into bed. It's only 10.30. Wow, I might be able to get six hours of sleep tonight.

The night goes by uninterrupted.

FEAR OF FLYING
(AMONG OTHER THINGS)

ANOTHER SHIT MONDAY???? WHEN THE ALARM GOES OFF AT 5.42, I'm a little disgruntled. I can't remember what day let alone what state I'm in. Nevertheless, I hop out of bed and into the shower. I do my usual Monday beauty rituals, complete with home eyebrow tweaking and put my hair up in a knot while I do crunches. I decide to wear something outrageous today, subconsciously thinking it may help me take on the day. I settle on this new Prada outfit I got. It's a bright pink short leather skirt and jacket with little mirrors stitched in. The shirt, if you can call it that, exposes my belly button, a big no-no, and is white with pink stitching. I have a pair of five-inch bright pink Steve Madden platforms that completes the look. I am definitely an eyeful.

I blow-dry my hair stick straight and use a smoothing wax to piece it together and spike it down. I go really heavy on my eye makeup and line my lips with a very pale pink. I look like I should be on the runway. Uh oh. Watch out now. I curse myself for applying lipstick so early because now I can't drink a bottled water without messing it up. I simply don't have time to re-apply. It doesn't matter. The sun is shining and I'm on my way.

In history, everyone is staring at me. I love the attention, though I caught this one cliquey-type bitch checking herself out in one of the mirrors. We don't do shit all class. The teacher's got about a million videos, so we're watching one now on Eisenhower. And people wonder how I can keep my grades up missing so much school.

Psychology is the worst ever. Today we're discussing development and Grendel makes us watch part of *Bambi*. Yes, I am predisposed to hating this movie, having gotten in a catfight with a bitchy blond model named Bambi before, but still the movie has no place for psych class. Everyone is awing and cooing at the TV and I am getting more and more nauseous. I can't be bothered to wait to get his attention so I get the hell out of there and head into the bathroom. There's nothing in my stomach to throw up but I do manage a few dry heaves.

French is decent. We go around talking in small groups. Madame loves my outfit, having seen something quite similar in last month's copy of French *Vogue*. Was I in that issue? Anyway, having that class puts me in a better mood.

Landed

And as for Hitler? I am not concerned. I don't go to his class. For once he's not here. I bet he's out creating his own Aryan race out of Twinkies...fat fucker. Plus, Slutstitute is there and seeing her that close to lunch makes me ill. So whatchya gonna do?

I just hang out in my car until lunch shift and then go and hang out with Shaz and Leigh. Kirby's not with her today – complete shock – so the three of us actually get a table to ourselves. That's a shocker. Shaz is wearing a long black matte skirt from Nieman's with two huge slits up the side. She's also got on this tunic top by Ralph Lauren in white, oatmeal and black. It looks very elegant and cool. Total contrast to me. Leigh, on the other hand, is wearing cargo pants and a melon-colored cotton shirt, both by Balenciaga's, I think. We certainly make a trio. They both have lunch, I, on the other hand, abstain and then the bell rings for class.

Leigh's got a drafting class she has to go to and me and Shaz have honors English. I fill Shaz in on what Fielding said on my machine last night. She can't believe it.

'Are you for real?'

'I'm serious, Shaz, why would I make that up? I mean, I was surprised too. I hate when teachers meddle in my personal life and act all anal.'

'God, I know. Remember how last year she thought I was suicidal. I would have killed myself just to get out her class.'

I chuckle. 'Or when she told me she was worried I was developing an eating disorder when my Calvin Klein ad came out. What a bitch.'

We walk into the room and take our respective seats. Fielding is wearing a hideous bandana dress straight out of *Oklahoma*. Plus, her shoes are this foul shade of red, picture an anemic tomato; I feel like retching. This guy, Joe, in my class sees me make a face and he starts laughing. We have kind of a camaraderie in English class, although I never hang out with him outside of that. Shaz likes him too. He always cracks jokes about Fielding and sometimes he threatens to grenade the other side of the room.

Our classroom is constructed much like a caste system. On one side in the back are the untouchables, and gradually it progresses to the despots. Me and Shaz and an elitist few. Shaz is always fucking with Joe. He's kind of one of the people in 'the group' but not really. The 'group' being the popular bunch in our school who chill and stick annoyingly close together. Not that that's a bad thing, but intentionally or not they make other people feel really bad. Most of the people in it are pretty dumb and I think that's why Joe and Shaz get along; they're both not.

Joe's pretty aggressive to say the least. He comes from this long line of wealthy Italians. So I mean we have to call him Don and sometimes Godfather. He was dating this girl for a really long time but when their relationship ended he hadn't really let go. Some asshole moved in on her and fucked around and Joe saw him in the hall one day and went berserk. He took the guy by the neck and threw him against a locker. He started beating the guy senseless. It was pretty funny. I almost got shoved in because it happened when I was walking to chorus. Everyone's lucky I didn't. I was carrying pepper spray.

Meanwhile, English is droning on. I can't pay attention. I shoot Fielding with one of my iciest glares and at the end of class she comes up to me. 'Is something wrong, Gwen?' she asks, in this real sugary voice.

'Uh, not really. Why?'

'Oh, you seemed kind of distracted today in class. I was wondering if something might be wrong at home?'

'No,' I say, vehemently. Damn, I just wanna say, the only thing wrong is how you teach your bloody class.

'Oh, OK, then. Don't forget your paper is due tomorrow.'

'Um, Miss Fielding, I turned it in today because I won't be back till Friday. I have a shoot in LA tomorrow. I'm leaving early in the morning.'

'Gwen, aren't you worried about missing so much school?'

Aren't you worried about your lacking sex life and cellulite-covered thighs?

'Not really, Miss Fielding, I always get the work made up.'

'Well, all right. But remember what I said about participation points.'

'Yeah and remember what I said about Fashion Emergency,' I say under my breath.

I walk out the door where Shaz is waiting. I go to trig and then leave. Frankly, I'm not concerned. I go home and change and go work out.

At the Y I am met by a new horror, Vile Bitch. Vile Bitch is a woman of ambiguous age, though I'd venture to say mid-thirties. She, like Preteen Slut, wears sportsbras and Spandex which all but cover her pale flabby gut and dimple thighs. Not only this, but she also has a large amount of hair growing other places on her obtrusive body besides her head. I cannot stay here. Thank God, I'm leaving tomorrow. I better go pack.

Back at home my room is an absolute sty. I've gotta decide on the perfect outfits to take, and in LA I never know what's going on. I take four suitcases full of clothes, one full of makeup and hair products and a bag full of pharmaceuticals and drink. Even the drink's risky. Leigh doesn't want me taking any contraband because she's afraid it won't get through baggage claim. Please, I keep my bowl on me at all times. I could even wear it around my neck. It practically looks like a Tiffany. No one would be able to tell.

Even with all my bags packed I can't sleep. I'm nervous about this whole campaign. This is the first time I've ever worked with Riley on a shoot before. My feelings are all jumbled up inside. On the one hand, I wanna get with him. I wanna know what it's like to care for somebody like that, but on the other hand I'm too scared. It's like I'm afraid that if I touch him, he'll to turn to shit. Everything else in my life has. I don't know what to do. I pop five over-the-counter sleeping pills and start to drift off. I shouldn't have gotten the over-the-counter kind. They give you the weirdest dreams...

So I'm sitting in LA...or at least that's what I think it is. It's on this beach and the water's blue, the sand's white, it's beautiful out. OK, so maybe it's not LA. But there's camera crew everywhere and me and Riley are alone on this beach. Everybody's watching us from above on this dune, and that's where they're all taking pictures. So we're doing all sorts of weird poses and laughing and splashing around in the water and all of a sudden this giant jellyfish emerges and grabs on to my leg. Riley starts yelling, but he's not yelling out of concern, he's yelling out of anger.

'What the fuck is this? God, Gwen, this is exactly like you to screw everything up when the photo shoot was going so well. Why'd you have to bring this thing here? 'Go on, just get out of my sight. I can't work with somebody as unprofessional. Why don't you just fucking leave!'

He storms off and I can't talk. The water gets colder and colder and I go deeper and deeper underneath. Then I see

Shaz and she's a mermaid except she's got this platypus-like beak and she's quacking at me and everybody's just watching me sink deeper and deeper and nobody's helping...

My alarm awakens me up from this undersea hell at precisely 4.32. My plane leaves at six and Leigh and I want to get there at least ten minutes before take-off. I'm kind of sweaty from my dream and a little discombobulated but I wash away my fears in the shower. I add a moisture-intensive mud pack to my hair and rinse it out. Then I blow-dry my hair straight on the high-heat setting to activate the thermal power of the treatment. My hair looks great. It's supposed to be in the 80s in LA so I should dress appropriately. I have this skimpy dress by Comme des Garçons. It's pale grey and slightly below the knee. I have some very strappy black sandals that go really well with it. I'm elegantly and appropriately bursting into spring.

I don' t eat breakfast because I don't have time (keep telling yourself that, Gwen) and everything is all packed and by the door just as Leigh and her dad arrive. Leigh's dad is nice enough to drop us off at the airport in his Expedition. We need a huge car to cart all of my – I mean our – shit. To her credit, Leigh has only one large suitcase, a backpack, and a carry-on bag. I am suitably impressed. I feel sort of embarrassed, but I quickly get over it. Leigh cannot be spoken to first thing in the morning. She's usually looking rough this early but today she looks great. She's wearing a pair of putty-colored Three Dot flat-front slim-fit khakis and a lavender twin set by Plenty. She's drinking a cup of coffee and I'm staring wistfully at it but I can't drink it on account of my teeth.

We get to the airport and the same old people help us in. Leigh kisses her dad goodbye and she's finally starting to perk up. To her dad's credit, we arrive fifteen minutes before departure which gives us ample time to load up. This time there's no question as to how many carry-on bags I can take. I made sure Tyrone called US Air after the last incident. We're boarded on the commuter flight and in a blink we're in Philadelphia.

I don't know how Tyrone managed but he got us a non-stop flight to LA. I am stoked, let me tell you. I hate layovers and nothing is worse than being laid over in the morning, when it's considered socially unacceptable to drink. Leave it to me to break the taboos. I decide after taking off that now is as good a time as any, and I have a heart to heart with Leigh about my situation with Riley.

'All right, Leigh, I'm gonna get your read since you've been my best friend forever. What am I supposed to do about this whole thing with Riley?'

'Who the fuck am I, Joyce Brothers?'

'No one likes a smartass. I'm being for real. Please, this whole thing with him has been causing me a lot of suffering. I really do like him, but I also have these weird feelings inside. I thought I'd be able to talk about it with you. Shaz is great, but half the time she's off in her own little world with Chris and you know it. I knew once she discovered sex she'd be unstoppable, but c'mon.'

Leigh cracks a smile.

'And, I mean, I don't know. I like Riley, but I'm afraid. See, I can like people and not really have feelings. I can fuck them and hang out with them but they may not mean that much to me. It's not like my relationship with you or Shaz at all. I'm afraid Ri wants something on a much more intimate basis. And I don't know if I can give him that. I have enough trouble maintaining partial sanity as it is. I don't know how well he can see that. I want to be up front with him but I don't know how he'd take it. What would you do?'

Leigh pauses and looks at me, reflecting. 'I'm trying to think of what you can do. I've known you forever, so I know your little quirks and I accept them. It's who you are. I don't know if Riley knows the real you, or just some peripheral vision he sees breezing in and out of shows. I mean, how many people know the real you? Like three? But the real you is great. It's worth getting to know. Behind that snobbish exterior is a wonderful person that nobody really gets to see.' She tweaks me. 'And I think if you feel it could work, you should give Riley a try. Gwen, you give this air that you're more sophisticated than the rest of us. You wear all the right clothes, drive the right car, have the right house, etc.... You're the envy of a lot of people. You're a hell of an actress. People can't understand why you're so unhappy. When people hear me talk about how miserable you are, they think I'm joking. Seriously. It's because people don't see the real you and see the insecurities that you try to cover up. With me and Shaz they're exposed, but to the rest of the world there's this mask of a frigid, unfeeling, beautiful demi-god that is Gwen. The mask is a defense. You've got to trust people and bring them into your circle and expose yourself. Not literally, of course.' She laughs lasciviously. Leave it to Leigh to lighten up the moment.

'You really think so?' I was stunned. I had no idea Leigh had this kind of deep perception. Damn all those personality analysis books she's been reading. 'So you think I should give Riley a chance?'

She looks at me for a long time with clear blue eyes. I'd kill for her eyes. 'No,' she says slowly, 'I didn't say that. I said I think you should give someone a chance.'

Leigh and I don't really talk anymore for the rest of the plane ride, as shocking as that may seem. What if she was right? What if I do give this mask to people? But should I let them in? I don't know what I'm so afraid of. All in all, it's food for thought, and that's good because that's the only kind of food I've been having.

LA OR BUST (34C)

THE PLANE LANDS IN LOS ANGELES AIRPORT A LITTLE earlier than expected which to me is fantastic. My ass was so asleep it was hibernating. Leigh is rejuvenated after an invigorating pee and both of us are ready to go out and have some fun.

Again there's a taxi cab waiting to pick us up. I was afraid that, being LA, there would be some strange Mexican man, still in sombrero and reeking of beer, waiting to drive us off south of the border. Luckily we just have an average-looking woman of about fifty with graying hair and shrunken features. She doesn't say much the entire trip. In fact, she knows where we're headed; I guess Ty had filled her in. I'm glad because I have no idea where we are staying.

It turns out we have a suite at the Beverly Hills Hotel. I'm

Landed

happy. Aw, this is my favorite, absolute favorite, place to stay in LA. The pink building reminds me of the Barbie dream houses of yesteryear, God bless 'em. As it turns out, all the models are staying here and we're all on the same floor. I check as soon as we get in to see if Riley has arrived but he hasn't. For some reason that makes me feel a little relieved. I wanna go out tonight and Leigh is anxious to have an evening alone with me checking out the LA scene without any others tagging along. I know what she means, I hate being the third wheel.

By the time we get settled and unpacked it's almost seven. I so want to eat at Spago while I'm in town, but unless I can get in touch with a celeb friend of mine admittance is gonna be impossible. Wolfgang has never been known to pull me any strings. Leigh has this craving for enchiladas so we ask people at the front desk to give us the name of a really good Mexican restaurant. The lady steers us in the direction of a place called La JaGringos which is supposed to be good, so we get a cab and head off.

La Ja doesn't accept reservations, of course, and there's an hour wait but we decide to stick it out. We get our IDs ready and mosey up to the bar. I order a dirty banana and Leigh gets a piña colada. We're chilling at the barstools sipping our drinks when these nasty guys start hitting on us.

This one guy with blond short spiky-tipped hair with horrible roots and too many earrings puts his arm around Leigh.

'You're certainly a nice little creature. Damn, baby, I wouldn't mind being the straw you're sucking.'

Leigh doesn't even flinch. 'Of course you wouldn't mind, but that's wishful thinking. Even this three-inch straw is better hung than you could dream to be. Now wait a minute, I had something else to tell you. What was it...oh man, oh yeah, I remember. Fuck you, that's it.' She crosses her arms.

The guy is shocked. He and his friends slink away. Leigh doesn't say anything. I don't understand. I think I must be wearing a sandwich board that says nasty guys accost me. Please, I can't even begin to tell you how much it bothers me. Leigh just laughs and says don't worry, she likes the chance to show off her wit.

We're finally seated. I order a rice, bean and pepper medley, two more dirty bananas, oh, and a San Pellegrino. Leigh gets cheese enchiladas and a peach daiquiri. While our food is being prepared we discuss her relationship with Kirby. She's happy with the way things are going. I don't think she intends to stick with him in college but she's glad they're having fun right now. I tell her I empathize and she's lucky she's got somebody caring who she can chill with but not get too attached to. She nods her head in agreement.

The food gets here. It's all right. Mexican food doesn't really do it for me. The drinks are good, but I pick at my dinner. Leigh scarfs hers up. I envy her in a way. She can eat whatever she feels like eating and it doesn't bother her. She's in good shape and she's very, very healthy. She doesn't have the mindset that food's the enemy. She's lucky.

Meanwhile, this restaurant is turning very white trash. We agree that we should go dancing and head off to an underground club scene called The Warehouse.

It's a pretty cool place. I like it, so does Leigh. There's a lot of good-looking people here and not really much of a weird element. This is where the Hollywood kids hang out I guess. God, I haven't seen this much coke in one building since I visited Coca-Cola headquarters in Atlanta. It's absurd. People are snorting left and right. I am not into the uppers, plus Leigh and I have quite a nice buzz going on, so we don't feel there's the necessity to do anything else. We dance together and with a bunch of people we don't know too. It's unbelievable. I've never had this much fun at a club before in my life. We stay until about 2.30 and then decide to return to the hotel.

I don't have to get up early tomorrow, bless Him. They don't want the models until about four to start setting things up. The crew is gonna be there first thing getting ready, but the light's best at sunset so we'll probably shoot between six and 8.30. We have to do about five changes for this spread, some pictures of which are gonna be used for billboards, posters etc. I'm excited.

We get back to the hotel room and there are roses on one of

our beds. I rush over to them, thinking they're from Riley, and the note attached is to Leigh from Kirby. How bloody sweet. I have to piss from all that alcohol. I get into the bathroom and fumble for the light switch. Something smells sweet. I turn on the lights and see two dozen yellow and pink roses covering the marble sink. On the mirror written in pink lipstick is:

HAPPY RETREAT, GWEN. CONSIDER MY OFFER – ♡ **RILEY.**

Damn! He has to do something like this. Leigh comes in and starts squealing. 'Forget what I said on the plane, Gwen,' she exclaims. 'He's definitely the one.'

OK, so I've gotta admit, these flowers give Riley definite brownie points. At first, I was a little taken back by the message on the mirror being that it was in lipstick. Sorry, I didn't know if it was my color or not. Luckily, it's a pink that even Fielding wouldn't be caught dead in.

I talk it over with Leigh and I think it's best not to say anything to Riley until tomorrow. Leigh disagrees but she always makes rash decisions. This whole gift thing makes me think about what Leigh and I talked about on the plane. I'm wondering if I should give him a chance. What's the worst that could happen? No, I better not even ask that since it'll just prep me to expect that. Well, I get in bed and konk out. It's been an emotionally exhausting day.

*

Landed

Leigh's still asleep when I wake up. I intend to keep it that way. She turns into a psycho bitch if she gets woken up before she has to. I slip into some Tommy Gear athletic wear and head down to the hotel's gym. God, it's great. They've got nautilus and free weights and a whole room of cardio. I'm in heaven. I work out for almost two hours, doing leg and back, and an hour of cardio. I'm drenched when I leave so I hurry back upstairs to shower.

I can't believe it but Leigh's still asleep. She's such a lightweight! Oh well, I'll let her. I take a brisk, twenty-minute shower and shave, exfoliate and smooth my various body parts and then I'm ready to blow-dry my hair. It's a pain in the ass because when I do these campaigns they usually want me to come to the shoot with my hair at least semi-straight. That's the look this year, you know: long, straight hair. Plus, it's gonna be windy and humid by the water so I've gotta account for that. I use the biggest round brush I have and a super-relaxing balm to get my hair totally stick straight. I have to admit, it looks pretty good. I shouldn't wear anything too nice since I'm gonna have to change so I put on a really short pair of flax-colored shorts by Lucy Love and plunging cornflower-blue T by Shameless. I also put on a pair of mules with a very clunky sole since I need to be comfortable walking around.

By the time I get all this done, it's nearing three o'clock. Leigh's up and she says while I was showering somebody called saying I need to be ready by 3.15 instead of at four. Hmm, glad she told me. Leigh's coming with me to the shoot, at least to get some sun, so she needs to get ready too. That freaks me out but I remember she takes absolutely no time at all to shower.

She's done in a matter of ten minutes. Her hair's wet, so she's got on this contoured straw hat with her hair all tied up beneath it. She has on this phat bathing-suit top that's black with light blue piping and a tank over that. And she's also wearing cut-off Abercrombie jeans. She looks very fresh, like she practically lives here.

So we're all set. The other models are all out in the lobby... we're the last ones there. I don't recognize anybody else in the campaign except for Riley. They've tried to make it really diverse. There's this beautiful black girl named Gloria. She's like 5 feet 9 inches and has a really smooth, caramel-colored complexion. She has curly hair cropped close to her head. Her features are perfectly proportioned. I wonder why I haven't seen her before. She seems really nice. Hopefully, this'll help her career take off.

The other two guys beside Riley are really different-looking. One's 6 feet. He's got long blond hair that's kinda straight, kinda wavy. He's really tan and surfery-looking; he probably lives in California. The other guy is half white, half oriental, so he's got those really high cheekbones and medium brown hair. His eyes are kind of slanted but not exaggeratedly so. He's the tallest of Riley and the California guy. He seems pretty nice too.

There's one other girl there. She's got chin-length brown hair and a lean, muscular body. I recognize her from a *YM* spread two months ago. I think her name's Tara.

I find out the guys' names are Scott and Jaret. Scott's the surfer dude. As it turns out, he's Riley's friend who's living with us in the summer. I can tell already from the small talk we've made that he's a genuine person and real easy to talk to. I can see Leigh checking him out already. Watch out, girl, you're married.

We're doing the group shot first since that's gonna be the hardest. This lady, Stacey, with the clipboard tells us that they've also picked a guy and a girl to be featured individually for separate ads. I'm shocked because she announces Riley's name and my name. Riley grabs me and picks me up. He gives me a really deep kiss that I'm surprised to find myself returning. Stacey laughs and says, 'I can see you two already know each other.'

And then I say, 'Nah, this is the first time we've met.' Everybody smiles and we all pile into this big van that's gonna take us to the location. I have to sit on Riley's lap which worries me because I don't want him trying any funny business. There's one odd person left without a seat besides me. Tara was gonna deal with it, but Leigh insisted she have her seat. How kind. She really wanted an excuse to sit on Scott. He's already tickling her and flirting with her like they've known each other for ages. I wish I had a camera.

The van ride lasts almost an hour. I am getting restless. Plus, Riley's got this monster hard-on which I can feel pressing into the back of my thigh each time I shift around. It's not exactly the most comfortable feeling. But everybody is in a jovial mood and we're all singing and laughing. I've never felt this much bonding between a group before; even Leigh is having fun. We're all kind of sad when the van finally pulls up to the private beach and we have to begin shooting.

We each have several outfits to model in various scenes. I get a white tankini which they rip so you see a large portion of my belly, white linen pants and a camisole-like top. And also a three-quarter-length red gingham shirt and denim capris. We do the swimwear part first.

I was wrong. The hairstylist didn't care if my hair was straight or not since it was gonna get wet anyway. She does add a bunch of waterproof makeup but other than that they turn us loose. All the girls are wearing skimpy bathing suits. Tara has this black one-piece with the Tommy logo and Gloria gets this bright blue boy-cut bikini. All the guys are totally ripped. They're all wearing board-style shorts and various beaded neck-laces. The cameras are set up by the water so they tell us to start off playing tag and then just to mess around.

I am having so much fun. Leigh is watching, cracking up

as I get dunked like countless times. At one point, my left breast just pops out of the suit but I'm laughing too hard to care. It takes about an hour but they finally get the shots they need after taking six rolls of film. Next, I put on the gingham and the capris. We all do this photo where we're lying on the sand laughing with the various guys holding the girls. That change doesn't take too long, and then I have my final outfit.

This is the one that Riley and I are doing together, by ourselves. He's cleaned up and is wearing really baggy light-colored flat-front chinos and a Tommy madras long-sleeve shirt. Both the pants and the shirt are rumpled and faded-looking and the sleeves and cuffs are rolled up. He looks really good. The stylist fixed my hair so it's straight again and she put some kind of tonic in it so it's incredibly shiny.

They tell us to pretend we're a couple which isn't exactly that hard and roll around on the sand together. Riley pushes me and we start play-fighting and fall down. The photographers are yelling, 'Perfect! C'mon, keep it up!', etc. It's kind of inspiring. We're both out of breath, smiling for the camera, and the director tells me to move in like I'm whispering something to Riley. At first, just to be a tease, I stick my tongue in his ear, but they laugh and say, 'Cut that out.' They tell me to pretend like I have something really important to tell him, but just say whatever into his ear. I hold my breath. Should I do it?

'Riley, I've decided... Thank you. Thanks for being you. I do want a relationship.'

Riley smiles extra big, his eyes are shining.

'CUUTTTTTT!!!' the photographer yells. 'Great. That's a wrap.'

All in all the shoot was successful. I'm certainly happy. Me and Leigh and Scott and Riley decide to shower back at the hotel and then go out to dinner. I know I've made the right decision about Riley, I'm actually hungry.

Once we get back to the hotel room, I attack Leigh. She's positively glowing. 'Leigh, ohmigod. You like him. You totally 100 percent have fallen for this surfer guy you just met.'

She can't stop smiling. 'Stop it, I know. I feel great. It's like I used to feel with Kirby.'

Oh man. In the interim I hadn't really thought about him. 'Leigh, that's great and all, but doesn't that sort of bother you? I mean, you just got back with Kirby and everything.'

She sighs, 'OK, don't get mad, Gwen, please. Because I know you weren't exactly thrilled the last time I wasn't 100 percent truthful. All right, see that night at the party, after me and Kirby fucked, I realized something had changed. Something significant. He realized it too. We both kind of decided that it would be best if we chilled for a while and to, you know, have some space. We're both so happy now. The reason I didn't tell you or Shaz is because I thought you would go off at me for making such a big deal about getting back together with him and then breaking up, etc.... Jesus, I'm just like a yo-yo. But, a few days ago, we talked and we both agreed we were much better off just staying friends. I still love him. Just not in that way, you know? Are you mad?' She looks really scared, like I'm gonna yell at her.

'Oh, God, no. Leigh, honey, I'm relieved. I was starting to worry about your whole thing with Kirby in addition to my other problems. I was having an even harder time getting to sleep. But I am surprised. I thought you were back all strong again. I'm not upset though. If this is what you want. Hell, yeah! Go for it with Scott. Just don't get too attached...or you'll end up like me.'

'Hah, hah. I didn't think you were gonna have anything to do with Riley, even after the flower ordeal.'

'I changed my mind.' I tell her about what happened at the end of the shoot. She runs up to me shrieking and gives me a big hug. You'd think I'd won the lottery. I shake her off and laugh. I yell at her to get in the shower since we have to be ready in little more than an hour. She swats me with a towel but complies.

I lie on my bed and hug a pillow. Oh man. Is this happy???

I'm still practically giddy when Leigh comes out of the bathroom. It's really a weird feeling, even better than the high end of bipolar. I don't know why, but all of a sudden it's like something's finally right. It's not a side effect from my medicine, so don't even...No, I mean, I took everything today. Whatever it is, I hope it doesn't go away.

I glance up at Leigh...wow, she's gone through a total transformation. Normally, she hates dressing up but I guess Scott has changed that. Her hair is straight and smooth. It's hanging really heavy on her shoulders and looks very healthy. Maybe she used a mask. She's wearing a golden-colored sleeveless shirt by Laundry and a short black skirt with mini slits up both sides. This is probably the best I've seen her look. She sees me staring at her, holding back a laugh, and says, 'Aw, fuck it, Gwen. I can look good if I want to.'

I shrug and grin. 'Whatever floats your boat.' I push her out of the way and run water for a shower because I stink.

In the shower, I shampoo and detangle and use a perfumed shower gel to loofah my body. I blow-dry my hair straight and put in a reconstructive conditioner to help lessen some of the damage from the wind, sun and salt water. I carefully select my outfit since we're going somewhere nice. I decide on a short, skin-tight dress by Alaia that's white with a silver thread dispersed throughout the fabric. Also I have a pair of white and silver Ferragamos which complete the look.

Leigh and I are so incredibly nervous. You'd think this was

our first date or something, er, wait, technically it kind of is. I resolve not to treat Riley any differently. And I shouldn't. I mean, nothing's changed. It's just that now we're officially together. Oh wait, they're knocking at the door.

Scott steps in and he's a hell of a lot better than Kirby. His hair is in a ponytail and he's wearing black pants and a tight white V-neck shirt, Calvin Klein, I think, and this black shirt jacket. I know Leigh is probably just dripping.

Riley's got on this Sandy Dalal linen shirt and this funky pair of Issey Miyake black pants. We all seem so avant-garde.

They've arranged for a limo to pick us up and take us to…you guessed it, Spago. Shut up, I know. I practically scream when I find out. I can't believe it. I ask Riley how he got us in and, evidently, Scott's good buddy is a busboy there. I dunno, something about changing names on reservations. Whatever. I'm not concerned. Especially since this is gonna be a great night.

Our limo's beautiful. It's not a stretch which is all right by me. It still fits my absurdly high standards. We climb in the back seat and pop open a bottle of champagne to celebrate. Screw Shaz and her contempt for passé drinks. She hates champagne, especially champagne kirs. Luckily, Leigh doesn't share her feelings. We toast each other and before we're halfway there, we've already downed the bottle.

So we're making small talk and I get some general impressions about Scott:

1. He's mild-mannered. Leigh loves that. I mean, she wants someone to talk to but she hates people who are so blatantly opinionated that they can't see others' perspectives. It's a wonder she's friends with Shaz.

2. He seems like an all-round nice guy. He's polite. His mama done taught him well. I'm impressed and my manners, at least in social situations, are impeccable.

3. He's interesting. When he's talking it's not just about like surf stories or some shit. I mean, he's up on humanitarian issues etc.... He actually has substance, something which a lot of us clearly seem to lack.

4. Finally, he's funny. That's the biggest. Guys just gotta have a sense of humor. Not only because he's dating Leigh (just joshing, baby) but if he's gonna live with us, I simply will not, and I repeat will not, tolerate any bores.

So I'm impressed. Kudos to Leigh for choosing him. And kudos to Riley for being friends with him. Jeez, Riley is racking up all kinds of brownie points. I wonder what his reward will be. I remember our last encounter, ahem, hand job, wait did I say that aloud? And I don't want the same thing repeated. Not to be crude or anything, but I certainly don't get anything out of slapping that thing around. Well, at least Flo's not here and I don't have to worry about her monthly visit for a while, thank God. Stop it, Gwen. Concentrate on food. You need to eat tonight. That's probably why you feel so weird. Lack of food. Not this I'm in lust bullshit. I'm probably coming down with rickets or scurvy like a goddamn pirate. Now all I need is the facial hair or an eye patch. Mmm, that's an appetizing thought. God, I'm rambling, I should say something. But no, Scott's talking about some friend of his who went to the Heidi Fleiss trial. Champagne always does this to me. I get so stream of conscious. Like the time I started moaning about honey being the natural sweetener because I saw the gummi bear smushed in on somebody's shoe. What, you don't get the connection? Oh, I put tea in my honey, shit, I mean honey in my tea. I am drunk. Anyway, the honey's always in one of those bear-shaped plastic containers...you know. Fuck it, man. I know what I'm talking about.

Oh, Leigh taps me on the shoulder. I guess we're here. Spago's nice, but a little disappointing. I was expecting, I dunno, like camera crews outside snapping pictures, but this isn't the Oscars. We're led inside by this French-sounding man and Riley tips him a $20. Pretty generous. He just keeps scoring points. I love the inside of this restaurant. Very modern and eclectic. It's packed, but that's to be expected. I look at the menu. What do I want? Being a strict vegetarian I settle on a sweet potato and pomegranate compote and endive and raddichio salad. Riley gets this pasta dish with crabmeat, artichoke hearts and pine nuts. Leigh gets prime rib – she's a real meat and potatoes gal. Scott gets a braised hunk of mahi mahi with mango salsa and fried leeks.

Conversation is pleasant. My initial nervousness is fading. Probably from the two Xanax I took in the bathroom. Man, they're starting to hit hard. I can barely keep my eyes open. Oh shit.

'GWEN!!!' I think that's Leigh screaming.

KNOCKED OUT NOT UP

I WAKE UP WITH A COLD CLOTH ON MY FOREHEAD. I'M IN MY
dress still, thank God, and not in some God-awful T-shirt.
Where am I? I think this is Riley's room. Yep, definitely,
there's his bags and shit's thrown everywhere. Aw, how sweet;
he made a neat little area just for me. My head is pounding
like a bitch though. I've never been in this much pain. What
happened? I think I'm about to find out. Riley, in a pair of
boxers and a T-shirt, is emerging from the bathroom.

'Awake yet, Sleeping Beauty?'

'Hey, Ri, what happened?'

'You passed cold out. It was actually kinda scary.'

'Ohmigod! I'm so sorry, we're you embarrassed?'

'Stop worrying about us. We hid you under the table.' I
glare at him. 'Just joking, Gwen. No, we explained to the

waiter that you were really tired and were hypoglycemic and you'd had a busy day.'

'That's not what happened though.'

'What do you mean? Leigh told me that's what was the matter.'

'Oh, she did...?' I ask kind of tentatively. Shit, he really doesn't know.

'Why?' He sounds worried, there's an edge to his voice. 'What really happened?'

'Nothing, Ri, forget about it.' I lean towards him and start kissing his face and then his neck.

'Gwen, stop. I'm being serious.'

I smile flirtatiously. 'So am I.' I reach for the zipper on the back of my dress.

'Gwen, Jesus fucking Christ!!! Do you not understand that I'm worried about you ! You can't always use sex as a way to get out of a problem. I had to carry you out of a fucking restaurant. Don't you think I at least deserve to know what's going on?'

'Riley, I don't want to talk about it!' Now I'm getting upset. This is exactly why I knew I shouldn't get involved.

'Gwen.' His voice softens. 'Please, I promise I won't leave. I'll understand, just tell me.'

I start crying. I don't know what to do. Should I leave? Or should I really tell him? I know his promises and everything but it's scary. I don't want to confront him with my issues, especially not now. There I go, being the black plague. I turn everything I touch to shit.

I start to get up but he pushes me down.

'Oh, God.' I smile bitterly through my tears. 'I never knew you to like it rough, shall I break out the whips and chains?'

He unwillingly cracks a grin. I seize the moment. I start kissing his eyes and in a second my dress is off and I'm putting his hands all over me. Now he can't stop. Before long, his boxers are off, and I'm breaking open the Trojan wrapper. I've gotta stop doing this. How much longer can I hold him off? Some girls are lucky. They just hold off sex. I have to hold off me.

Man, I have the fucking most awful headache ever. I'm sure I look like buttcrack too. Riley's asleep next to me, drooling. Typical. I get up without waking him and look in the mirror. I am a sight. My eyes are all red and puffy, I look emaciated (coming from me that's pretty bad), and my hair is all clumpy and matted together. Plus, I'm cold. After all, I am still naked and Riley's got the AC blasting on 40.

I find a piece of paper and take an eyebrow pencil out of my purse – burnt cocoa to be exact. I write Riley a nice note that says:

Greg Benjamin

Riley –

I feel like shit, I went to my room to clean off and recoup.
Thanks again for last night. (3X)!!!

Smooches – Gwen.

There. I place it on the toilet top where he'll be sure to find
it and quietly close the door to his room. I've got my dress from
last night and my makeup is all smeared and caked on me. I
must resemble Medusa, or someone even more hideous, Tori
Spelling. Ugh. I take the key and slip open the door to my
room. Knowing Leigh, she'll probably be asleep. Yep, she is.
Hold up. And who's this? Ohmigod. Lying next to her asleep is
Scott in the flesh, and I mean in the flesh. Damn, he may be
a model but he's not flawless. He's got a big red zit on his ass.
I don't need to see all this.

I hurry into the bathroom and start the shower. God, does
it feel good. I take extra care washing this morning. I have to
first put makeup remover on and then wash my face with a
cream cleanser. I use shower gel, a moisturizer and a special
rehydrating shampoo and conditioner. I feel so much better
now that I'm showered, I can't even begin to tell you.

Leigh and Scott are both up and clothed when I get out of
the bathroom. Leigh's wearing a big T-shirt and Scott's got on
just a pair of Calvin Klein pajama pants. Scott says a sheepish,
'Hi,' to me and kisses Leigh on the cheek before closing the

door behind him. Leigh's smiling and looks elated.

'Hey, *chica*, what are you so happy about? Did someone play with her new friend?'

Leigh sort of blushes. 'Shut up, Gwen.' God, she's gushing.

'Aw, I'm glad you guys hooked up. Scott seems really sweet. You all seemed to really hit it off. Do you like him?'

'Yeah, I feel great, he's so ... I dunno, he's so *him*.'

'Don't be so specific.' I roll my eyes. 'More importantly, is he good?'

She looks at the floor, then grins and slowly nods. I burst out laughing. 'Tell me all! I want details: length, width and duration.'

She fills me in. Wow, they were up later than me and Riley! When we're finished swapping sex tales I realize there's something else I need to tell her.

'Oh, and Leigh ...'

'Yeah?'

'Thanks for last night.'

She smiles knowingly and nods. 'No problem.'

I really don't need to discuss it any further. Leigh knows what I mean and knows I know. A lot of people wouldn't do that for me. In fact, many wouldn't think that lying is being a true friend. I can't confront my issues and Leigh realizes that. She's got her idiosyncrasies and so do I. Part of being friends is understanding and getting over them. I know this sounds clichéd but I've never felt as close to her as I do right now. She gives me a big hug and then says, 'I'd hug you some more but I really need to wash off the bodily fluids.'

I laugh and push her off me. 'Some of us are clean.'

She gives me a pointed look. 'And some of us never will be.' And with that she goes into the bathroom.

While she's showering I dress. I put on black capris and a tight black raw silk shirt by Miu Miu. It clings to my ribs and then flows out. It's open except it has a single metal clasp by my breasts. I don't put on any jewelry except for a silver David Yurman pendant and I have my earrings on of course. Two in my right ear and three in my left. I feel only about 100 percent better.

Leigh comes out of the bathroom wearing two towels, one around her body and the other turban style. I can't decide who she resembles more: Erykah Badu or *I Dream of Jeannie*. I go with the latter since she's apparently not black. She puts on a navy and violet floral sarong and cap-sleeved shirt by BCBG. Her hair dries straight naturally, so we don't have to worry about taking the time to blow-dry it. I'm glad because I wanna get on our way. Today's our last day in LA. I know, I know, short but sweet. Yeah, right. Besides I promised Leigh we would go shopping on Rodeo Drive and also to the Beverly Center. We simply must make Shaz jealous. That's not too

Landed

difficult, Shaz gets jealous incredibly easy.

Today is just gonna be us girls. I don't even think about stopping to see Riley. No, no. Leigh completely understands. We walk outside and it's beautiful. Maybe if we get done in time we can go to the beach and play some ball, but you can't rush clothes, you know. So we hail a taxi and go the fifteen minutes it takes to get to Rodeo Drive. I'm determined to spend $10,000 on new clothes. It shouldn't be that difficult. Leigh isn't too keen on real designer clothes so I'm sure hers will be a much more reasonable total.

After about an hour of shopping I have exceeded my limit. What can I say, clothes just look good on me. Leigh has found only two things, both from Valentino. One is this very short gray skirt and then she also bought a white short-sleeved shirt with these green and gray leaves on it. The day's still early so I suggest we go play volleyball and get our tan on. Of course, Leigh wholeheartedly agrees.

We go back to the hotel and change into our gear. I wear a halter-style top and thong bottom with Roxy board-shorts over it. Leigh has on board-shorts too but she's wearing a sports bra-style top by Speedo. We go downstairs and ask the people at the front desk where the best beach is to play volleyball. There is some heated debate but we finally find out. It sucks because it's a half an hour away plus we have to wait for fucking ever to get another taxi.

When we finally do arrive we can see it was worth it. The beach is seriously just wall-to-wall courts. They're all arranged by level, so some rows are for B-level players while some are professional. I mean Karch Kiraly might be out here for all we know. Leigh is mad because I wanna play against girls. My bad, I've had enough bad experiences with guys to last for a year so the last thing I wanna do right now is play against them. She relents, reluctantly, but we luckily get in on one of the women's AA courts.

The women seem friendly enough. They both look like they're in really good shape. One's named Kelly and the other is Donna. Donna looks like she's pretty butch. Oh well, I'm not concerned. We take serve and Leigh plays weak side and I pick up strong. We play really well. I'm surprised we have much continuity since we never get a chance to play beach together but we end up winning 11–7 after about forty-five minutes of play. Donna and Kelly are good sports. Then we play some others who just came down to watch. We win this game too. We just can't lose. I'm finding it hilarious but everybody on the sidelines is getting mad. Probably because we're the youngest and best-looking people out here. Oh well, not my problem.

Leigh and I agree that it's time we play against the guys. It's obviously gonna be a lot harder since they're guys. They're stronger, taller and the net's almost a foot higher, but we're ready. We go to a guys' A court and there's a two-game wait but we get to go on next since we're girls and oh so beautiful.

The guys playing are in their late twenties. They're decent-looking but they seem like assholes. It's apparent they don't think we can play. They give us serve and Leigh starts serving up floaters. After their third shank they try to step it up. They pass the ball pretty well and it's a decent set but I pack the shit out of him. Everybody on the sidelines starts cheering and Leigh cracks up. The guys look really pissed. It's still Leigh's serve but she gets a netball so they start serving. I'm like, c'mon, Leigh, no points, sideout right here. Sorry but I get so into this. They serve Leigh a bullet but she passes it beautifully. I set her three off the net and she gets a kill on a deep line shot. OK, so it's my serve. I give them an easy top spin and they put it up but we dig their hit and they make a stupid error.

We switch sides because it's 4–0 and one guy with short orange hair asks if we want to make a wager on the game. All the guys on the side are like, 'C'mon, man, that's fucked up, etc....' but Leigh and I look at each other and shrug. So I go to my bag and take out my wallet and I'm like, 'OK, how about $50?' They're like, 'Oh, how about if we win you've gotta go out with us?' I say, 'Fuck no. I mean, we're gonna win but I'm not even gonna honor that.'

So we settle on $50 and Leigh and I turn it up. I start Jump-serving and I get two aces. They get serve and start coming back but we get a sideout when Leigh dumps it over on two.

Greg Benjamin

The game goes on back and forth but we win after it's 10–9 on a roundhouse from Leigh which gets returned. Leigh sets me up for a two-ball and I miraculously hit a perfect line shot.

The guys are super pissed but pay up. By now, Leigh and I are drenched, thirsty and tired. We buy some Evian and hail a taxi and return to the hotel. It has been the best day.

BREAKING OUT... I MEAN BREAKING UP IS HARD TO DO

WHEN WE GET BACK TO THE HOTEL ROOM, I FLOP DOWN ON the bed. I am exhausted. Leigh and I want to do something cool tonight, being that it's our last night in LA. So I suggest we go our separate ways and she spend time with Scott and I with Riley.

Leigh's elated, I'm not. I still don't know what to do about Riley. I thought initially it was gonna be so much fun to be involved and have a real person to be with. But last night just cemented the fact that I'm a fuck-up, or black plague, whatever you wanna deem me. Now, Riley's even more intrigued with finding who the real Gwen is. That's a crock of bullshit. I mean, I need to break it off. Cool, huh. I've been with the guy for all of like eighteen hours. Just like a fucking bra. But meanwhile, it's still been enough time for me to realize that he's better off without me. Notice I didn't say I'm better off without him. That's still unestablished. I think I'll break it to him tonight at dinner. That way he can see the walking disorder in person.

Leigh calls Scott and they decide to go out clubbing. Leigh showers quickly because she wants to catch the happy hours at all the bars before it's too late. I wonder why she's so concerned about spending an extra buck or two per drink if she's not the one paying for them but I keep my mouth closed. I call Riley while she's in the bathroom and tell him to come over to my room in about an hour and we can decide what to do from there. He sounds excited but my voice is a little weary and I think he can read that. All of a sudden, I'm filled with this impending sense of doom. It's not the harbinger of a bad hair day, I don't think. It's not quite that potent, but something ominous is definitely lurking in the future. It's times like these when I wish my intuitive powers weren't so strong. They distract me from getting ready.

Leigh's already done showering and looks casually hip in a two-layer peach sundress by Guess?. For some odd reason she's meeting Scott downstairs and not in our room, so she rushes out the door after giving me a quick hug. I'm sad to see her go looking so happy. No, I don't want my friends to feel as bad as I do. But still, sometimes I wish I could be as carefree as they are. Life's a bitch though. And a mean one at that.

Landed

I shower and take extra preparations getting ready. I blow-dry my hair straight and arrange it in a carefully careless knot on the top of my head with wisps and tendrils poking out and along my face. I use a lot of matte makeup to appear spring-time fresh, as if I were doing a douche commercial. OK, sorry. But it does look very springy. I put on a form-fitting, white Vera Wang dress with yellow and pink flowers embroidered throughout the fabric. It's got thick straps and is cut about eleven inches above my knee. It's probably the longest skirt I have with me. My bad, I know, but I'm trying to appear whole-some and not like some sneaky ice-hearted bitch who chews guys up and then spits them out. Don't call me Estella.

I have a few minutes before Riley comes to collect myself. Luckily there's a minibar in our room, so I down a few shots of JD to calm my nerves before he gets here. Silently I curse myself. Now I can't have any Xanax. Not after last night. Oh well, I guess I'll have to go through the night a shaky mess. It won't be the first time.

Somebody knocks.

'Come in,' I call out tentatively. Riley comes in and he looks really good. He's wearing a baby-blue button-down Cynthia Rowley shirt and a pair of baggy linen pants by Jean Paul Gaultier. It makes me wonder why I'm going through with this anyway.

'Hey, baby. You look great!' He walks over and wraps his

arms around me, giving me a big hug and an even bigger kiss.

I guess I kind of tense up because he asks if something's wrong. I try to smile and shake my head but my acting is not up to snuff today. I believe it's because I haven't done too many commercials in the past month. He senses something's up and motions for me to sit down on the bed.

'Gwen,' he says, 'we never finished what we were doing last night.'

'Shut up. I thought you came twice!'

He smiles and shakes his head. 'You know what I'm talking about.'

'Riley, I'm not even gonna go there. C'mon, this is our last night in LA. Don't you wanna make this night special? I really don't want to drag you down.'

'Of course it's gonna be special. I'm spending it with you.'

Now don't groan. Ordinarily, I would gag, retch or even projectile vomit, but coming from Riley this sounded really sweet, even genuine.

'All right, Ri, I'll tell you. But first I've got to get something off my chest. As surprised as you're going to be to hear this, I'm sure . . . I don't frequently show my emotions. You don't know Shaz too well, but she's often the same way. She masks her feelings with sarcasm and big words. She's stopped doing that now, ever since she met Chris.

'When we first planned to hook the two of them up I don't

know about you but I had no idea that those kind of sparks were gonna fly. She talks about him constantly. She says he makes her feel whole. Don't laugh. I'm being for real. They're crazy about each other. And now we're not as close. We don't have the same intimacy we used to. We don't laugh as much or hang out or relate to each other as well. In a way, I hate her happiness.

'You know Leigh even less than you know Shaz. She was involved with this guy Kirby for a really long time and recently they broke up. So no, you don't have to call Scott the home-wrecker anymore. Leigh and I were best friends. Even closer than me and Shaz. When she started chilling with Kirby all the time you have no idea how much we grew apart. Shaz and I got closer but it wasn't the same. Leigh and I had a past. I never really realized how much I resented Kirby until after they broke up. He's a great guy, but I felt like he was driving a wedge between us. It sucks to be mad at your friends for being happy. It makes me feel like shit.

'Don't roll your eyes, I'm getting to the point. We've always been close. And yes, don't worry, I've always been attracted to you. But after New York, I started thinking about you more and more. Riley, you are a super guy. I mean, you know you're great-looking, so I don't need to tell you that, but you also have a substance that a lot of people I know don't have. I'm scaring myself by how close I feel to you.

'What's even scarier is that I think I know you, but you

don't know the real me at all. I know you're gonna want to start protesting and shit because you wanna get to know the real me. But I don't want you to. Please, please, please, do not take that the wrong way. You deserve much more than me. I can't give you what you need and I certainly don't have the strength to have a relationship.

'Riley, I've got a lot of problems which I don't know if you're aware of or not. Looking good has always come easy to you. It doesn't feel that way to me. I never feel satisfied with who I am or what I look like. Last night, I didn't pass out because I'm hypoglycemic, I passed out because I overdosed on barbiturates and alcohol. I haven't eaten anything in three weeks. It's not something I can control.

'I've been in therapy for the past two years and it's not doing shit! I'm on enough medication to kill a small horse. It's hard. In addition to all my issues, I'm carrying around this emotional baggage that I don't want to have to dump on anybody. Especially you. I care way too much about you to do that.

'What concerns me most though is that I'm afraid I'm gonna change. I've never been good at rolling with the tides. I fight everything. I've seen how much having someone serious has changed my friendships with Leigh and with Shaz. I don't want the same thing to happen to us again because of me. They're my rocks. They're like the one stable thing I have in my life right now. Next year they're both going away. I don't wanna lose my time that I have with them, the three of us together for a final time. I'm sorry.

'Leigh and I spent the day together today. We didn't do anything special, just shopped and hung out and went to the beach. Today was the best day I've had in probably a year. No one understands how good it is to feel normal, even if it's only for a few hours. Today really made me realize how shitty I always feel, and how I'm responsible for that. I'm always under this constant pressure it seems to perform or be somebody. I'm not even sure who I am.

'And no, it's not like I need to go on some sort of pilgrimage to the Orient to find myself, but I need to start somewhere, and I need to do it alone. Riley, I was so afraid of scaring you off, it was giving me an even harder time trying to fall asleep. I thought if you knew how fucked up the real me was, you'd hate me. I've gotta be myself and stop pretending. I hope you can understand.'

Riley sits there in a stunned silence. 'Damn, and I thought we were just going out to dinner.'

I laugh and give a sympathetic look. I feel cold. I look down and realize Riley has been holding my hand. My hand is clammy and sweaty and shaking. He looks at me with a softness still, even after all I just said.

I start to cry.

He puts his arms around me and we lie there for a while, just breathing, totally silent. He gets up and leaves the room.

CONTRADICTION, SANS CALVIN KLEIN

FOR SOME REASON I SLEEP ALL THROUGH THE NIGHT. I barely remember, but I think Leigh came in at about three and said good night. I envy her. She likes Scott a lot but I think she realizes that she only needs someone to have fun with, not a relationship. She's not growing too attached. She'll have all summer though.

Summer??!! Shit. I wonder if this whole thing is off with me and Riley not together. But what's to be expected? We never promised to be together all summer. Man, if our plans get fucked up because of this, I'm gonna be one pissed puppy. Oh well, I can't worry about it now. I have to get ready because we have a plane to catch.

I take a fairly quick shower and put a deep cleansing mask on to help get rid of all that makeup and dried tears. I try to begin today as a slightly new me. For starters I don't wear any makeup, I let my hair dry curly and I put on a pink flowered dress by Aloha. Our stuff is already packed, thank God, so I don't have anything else to worry about. While I was showering Leigh said goodbye to Scott. I guess I should say the same to Riley.

I walk down the hall to his room and knock on the door. He opens it. He looks pretty rough. It seems as if he hasn't slept and he's wearing what he wore last night.

'Hi,' I say.

'Hey.'

I walk over and give him a careful hug, like he might break. 'I'm sorry.'

'I love you, Gwen.'

'What?'

'I said I love you.'

'But…'

He puts his finger to my lips and then kisses them. 'Look, I know what you said last night, but I think we can make it work. You really got me to thinking and I want to give it a try. I don't care that you have problems, I care about you.'

'But, Riley, didn't you listen to what I said?'

'I heard you, Gwen. That doesn't mean I agree.'

'Look, I don't think now is the best time to talk about it. Can you call me tonight after I'm home and settled in? I've got a lot to think about.'

'Sure, baby.' He gives me a hug goodbye. 'Don't worry, whatever happens, I'll still care about you. It's not gonna fuck up anything for the summer.'

'Thanks. Goodbye, sweetie. It was fun.'

I let my gaze linger for a minute and then walk out of the room. I feel a little better after talking to him now. At least I know this won't permanently damage our relationship. I have a lot to think about.

Leigh's all ready so we board up and our taxi's waiting to take us to the airport. Bye, Los Angeles.

It seems like I'm saying goodbye to everything. The conversation with Riley last night totally opened up my eyes. It's like I could see myself from the outside, almost like a one-way mirror. I saw the way my life was heading in that downward spiral. It sucked. But the more I think about it, the more I'm willing to take a chance. I've been selfish. I think I'm caring about Riley by somehow sheltering him from the terror that is me. In reality, I'm protecting myself. I'm the one who's afraid of getting hurt. I'm not protecting him from shit. I need to give this relationship a whirl. Not because I owe it to Riley. I owe it to myself. I hate having these kind of epiphanous moments. They're double-edged swords. As I said, just like beauty.

Leigh and I don't talk awful much on the plane ride home. We both have homework and she's engrossed in a drafting

project she's doing for her architectural portfolio. We do talk
though about how Shaz is gonna shit when she finds out about
Scott. It's cute. I mean, can you imagine three couples
together under one roof? How are we gonna partition the
rooms? God, this will be interesting.

By the end of the plane ride, I'm feeling much better. I
attribute my violent mood swings of the past few days to jet lag
and lack of sleep. Come off it, Gwen, way to cop out as usual.
The truth is I'm scared. Maybe I only like the idea of Riley, as
Leigh said. I'm being unfair to myself by not giving him a
chance, I don't wanna screw up everything in my life by isolat-
ing myself entirely. Man, just like a glacier, beautiful yet cold.
Dammit, why does this always happen? I'm sick of feeling this
way. I'm gonna let Riley thaw me out.

As it turns out, Riley suspected something was up. Or at least
that's what he says. He's delighted that I want to give our relationship a chance and in a way so am I. He's coming down in
three weeks for graduation and says he'll have a big surprise
waiting. Uh oh, and what can that be? I better start with my leg
exercises.

I go to bed tonight, for the first time in a long while, feeling truly content.

I remembered to set my alarm, so it goes blaring off at 5.42.

The usual droning ring is actually a welcome relief this morning. I'm glad to be home. After my shower and crunches, I put on a butter-colored wraparound skirt and cream half-shirt by Givenchy. Just call me Dairy Queen.

I make an effort to eat something, so I grab a half of a low-fat protein bar and some water before heading off. Hey, old habits are hard to break, you know.

In school, people comment on my even deeper tan and I play off their compliments modestly. School is such a joke now. Classes are winding down. People are skipping left and right. I can never be bothered to stay. The only thing we're doing in any of my classes is preparing for exams, which I don't even have to take because I've maintained at least a B average all year. I think that's pretty commendable. My parents are suitably impressed. My teachers are happy because I turn in all my work on time. I think my English teacher is a little upset. Maybe she wants me to fuck up. She'll get over it. I'm on a positive kick now.

Right before chorus, I spot Shaz and we decide to head out to lunch instead of chilling in the cafeteria. So after our lunch bell rings, we sneak off to the parking lot and take my Benz to the bagel shop.

Shaz looks calmed and happy. Chris has been wonderful for her. She tells me he's coming for graduation too and he also mentioned something about a big surprise. I wonder if the guys are in on something together. If so, at least it won't be as kinky as I was expecting.

I actually order lunch and Shaz is surprised and bemused. She gets a health sandwich on a poppy bagel and I order a sprout and tomato sandwich on focaccia. I almost eat it all. Easy, crusher, I'm making headway. These things take time, you know. Shaz is proud and congratulates me and I accept her praise with the quiet modesty of someone who's been used to such words for years. We go back to school begrudgingly because we don't want to have to deal with English.

It makes me so mad because English truly used to be my favorite subject. All hope is lost now. I'm thrilled beyond belief there's only a few weeks left. I swear if I was faced with any more time, I might have to make those suicidal fantasies a reality.

Of course, we catch all the red lights on the way back to school so we're like three minutes late to English. Fielding tells us she doesn't know what to do because if we're over three minutes late to class she's supposed to write us up for an office referral. Shaz rolls her eyes and I start making the *Psycho* noises. I mean, please, it's not like we were smoking up in the bathroom, today. She glares at us and announces we have, surprise, yet another boring-ass compare-and-contrast assignment. That's right, Fielding, load us up with crap like two weeks before graduation. God forbid we don't exceed the quota by thirty-five assignments. Please.

This class puts me in a shit mood. I go to trig and barely make it through. Physics, please, I heard we were watching a movie so I'm outie. School is such a joke. I don't understand why they don't tell us that in the first place. I am so stoked about getting out it's not even a joke. I don't know if I'll ever look back.

I go home, change and go work out. I don't run into any of the nasties which places me in a slightly better mood. I'm glad things are starting to work out with Riley. That scene in LA gave me quite a scare. I hate when I'm not in control of my emotions. I swear, sometimes it's like I'm outside of my body watching myself fuck up. It's so surreal, like a dream almost. Yep, and no matter how hard I pinch myself I just don't wake up. I even have the scars to prove it.

I drive home with a sense of urgency. I have a feeling something's waiting for me. I check the mail and I get a few payments from jobs I've done and, lo and behold, along with the junk mail and bills is the key to our beach house. Hell, yeah! I totally forgot, the lease started yesterday. Oh no. Leigh, Shaz and I must do the honors and do them tonight.

I call Leigh and Shaz and both of them are all about spending the night. We decide to take my car and meet over at my house at nine. That gives us plenty of time to pack, get ready and for me not to eat. Heh, heh. Sorry, I'm still in that mentality. As I always say, whatchya gonna do?

Landed

I shower and wash my hair, tying it up while it's still wet. I put on a pair of ripped jeans and a cropped sweater by Cousin Johnny. The sweater's lightweight but it still gets pretty cold at the beach at night during this time of the year.

I'm astounded because both Leigh and Shaz are on time. We have to stop by a package store on the way to our place so I can use my ID to pick up booze. I get a liter of Malibu, a liter of Bacardi Limon, a pint of peach schnapps and some Skyy vodka. Please, I think that should hold us off for tonight.

It's about a fifty-minute drive to OC when there's traffic so we have some time to kill. It's been forever since the three of us have just hung out. I can't begin to tell you. Everyone looks casually cute. Leigh is decked out in Abercrombie: boycut jeans and a three-quarter-length A & F track-and-field shirt. I know, funny, because she doesn't do track and field, but who am I to complain? Shaz is wearing flare-fit cargo pants and a tight green V-neck shirt by Calvin Klein. As soon as I've gotten the liquor put back in the trunk, Leigh starts blabbing.

'So, I was talking to Scott, and he says he's got some sort of surprise planned out for me. Have either of you heard anything about it?'

Shaz and I look at each other.

'Um, I have no idea, Leigh. Riley said the same thing to me. At first I thought it was something all perverse and shit but then Shaz said that Chris had something special for her too.

And I doubt Chris would be all into that. Although, what about the whip, Shaz?'

Shaz turns red. 'Dumbass, I told you that was for my horse.'

I shrug. 'Hey, if that's what you call it.'

She smacks at me from the back seat and in trying to retaliate I almost veer off the road.

'Jesus H. Christ, you guys!' says Leigh. 'For my safety and your own, Gwen, keep your eyes on the road. Shaz, keep your hands to yourself.'

'Yes, Mother,' we both chime in.

We're pretty much quiet the rest of the way up there. Damn, there's mad traffic in south OC. We finally pull up to our place. It doesn't look quiet and empty.

'Ohmigod!' Leigh whispers. 'Somebody's inside. All right, I've got my mace.'

'Would you please settle down. I bet the landlady just left the lights on for us.' Of course, Shaz would say something like that, being the pragmatic one.

'Here goes...' I walk up the stairs and turn the key.

'SURPRISE!!!!' Scott, Riley and Chris jump out from behind a couch all holding beer bottles. 1 turn on the light so I can see them better and they're wearing togas. Oh, sweet lord.

'Hey, baby.' Riley comes over to me and gives me a ten-second kiss, hmm... *déjà vu*?

All around me the other couples are embracing and saying

their respective hellos. Everybody's in a jubilant mood. I guess so. Shaz hasn't seen Chris for a few weeks and Leigh didn't think she would see Scott for at least another month. Yeah, and I'm happy too. It's good to see Riley, God love him.

'Wait a minute, you guys, is this a permanent thing?' I ask, remembering the surprise they were talking about.

Riley answers first.

'Yep, we thought it would be kinda cool to get an early start. That way we could come to your graduation and corrupt you beforehand by forcing you to drink and skip school.' He grins evilly.

Scott and Chris both chime in, 'Yeah.'

I have to laugh. 'Well, twist my arm, you guys. If you say so.'

Of course, Leigh and Shaz are practically jumping up and down with excitement. Whatever. I can see Shaz already concocting lies to tell her mom as to what she'll have going on instead of school in the upcoming weeks. I'm not concerned.

Everybody kind of relaxes and the guys shotgun a few beers. Of course, I simply have to join in and before I know it I'm pretty much shitfaced. Riley and Scott have bought several cases of Corona and in addition to the liquor we have it's quite a bundle. I feel in the spirit of being generous and suggest we call some fellow seniors to partake in our merriment. I'm sure they'll be shocked and delighted and, after all, our principal is always talking about giving back to the class.

I call a friend who is in my French class named Sarah. For some odd reason she's home. I tell her what's going on and insist that she bring a few friends and come on down. The only stipulation is that they must be appropriately dressed. After all, this is a toga party. Sarah is very happy to come and she promises to round up the cream of the crop. Hopefully it won't be too painful.

In the next forty-five minutes we haul ass to prepare the house. After everything is all set up and decorated, we make some makeshift togas out of sheets. Mine is beautiful. It's made from a 200 count Ralph Lauren pima cotton yellow sheet and I fold it so it even has an empire waist. Shaz is sporting a very skimpy toga with a floral pattern by Laura Ashley Home. And Leigh, the traditional, goes with the normal style and a classic gingham print by Horchow Home collection. By now we're all smashed.

We're just sitting around talking and basically giggling foolishly when the doorbell rings. I look outside. Shit, there's only like six additional cars outside. Oh well, ask not, want not. I open the door and in comes Sarah, followed by her boyfriend, Mariana, three of their friends and some other guys from our school who I don't know too well. I tell everyone to make themselves at home and soon everyone is drinking and having themselves a merry old time. But what can you expect, it is my party.

Someone has the audacity to start playing rap music. I

almost fall on the floor. Luckily, before I can find out the culprit, someone switches it to Dead and everyone kinda mellows out and just chills. I'm half tempted to call Sandee and invite her, but I know she wouldn't come. Oh well, I dial her number anyway.

'Hello,' a raspy female voice answers.

'Sandee?'

'Yeah, what?'

'Babe, it's Gwen. What are you doing?'

'Uggghhh, Gwen, what the hell are you doing calling so late? Vince'll kill me!'

'Aw, screw him, Sand. Guess where I am?'

'Oh, I don't know.'

'I'm at my new house.'

'That's just great.' She doesn't mask her sarcasm well.

'Listen, Sandee, you better come over here, we're having a party.'

She practically explodes. 'You better get the fuck out of here! You're full of crap! I am *not* driving all the way into Ocean City to come to an f-ing teenage party. You're crazy!'

'Sandee,' I say calmly, 'you *are* coming.'

'You better get out of town.'

'Sandee, I'm sending a cab.'

'Gwen, you better not.'

'I'll see you soon. Bye.'

Click. I hang up the phone. Screw it. It's all in good fun. I pick up the phone again and dial Ocean City Taxi. I give them Sandee's address and tell them I'll pay when they deliver her. That's fine with them. Sandee's gonna shit.

So I forget about that for a while. I play a few rounds of quarters and then we get in a circle and play I Have Never.

For those of you who haven't played, it is absolutely the most fun confessional game ever! I am not afraid to use the superlative either. You get in a big circle and everyone has a drink. One person starts it out and says I have never... and fills in that sentence, usually with something sexual, of course. If a person has done that thing they have to drink.

So we get in a large circle and I start out.

'I have never shagged in a bathroom.' I look around and no one takes a drink. No, no. I proudly take a swig. Everyone laughs. 'Lightweights!!!' I yell.

'My turn!' Shaz squeals. 'I have never given or received sexual favors in the back of a transit bus.'

She looks around. I pick up my bottle. 'What is this, pick-on-Gwen day? I swear to God, it's one of the reasons I never ride the bus. I almost choked.' People just think I'm the funniest person alive.

'I'll get her, Gwen,' Leigh says. 'I have never played role games with a lover when having intercourse or giving sexual favors.'

Landed

Shaz turns bright red but she and Chris both drink up.

The game continues. Everyone else around us is kind of boring. We did find out that Leigh has done the deed on a swing, in church, on a park bench, as well as done 'other things' in an amusement park. Wahey.

I don't even want to go into the things Shaz has done. My God, that would take up a book. Let's just say, she's certainly not shy when it comes to such matters. After we've all kinda finished the game, everybody is starting to drift off. Luckily, there are some DDs so not everyone has to stay at my place. Sarah and a few others stay but everyone agrees that this is the best party they've been to all year, and possibly ever. Hey, what can I say?

I go up to my room with Riley and we make out but we're both too drunk to have sex. I'm not upset. There will be plenty of time for that this summer. Believe you me.

It's weird. Tonight was a success. In a way it makes me regret distancing myself from everyone. I always felt people had this terrible perception of me. I think they were just intimidated. But this isn't some kind of enlightenment. I still wouldn't trade my friendships for anything. Certainly not to be in some clique. Not at all.

I glance at the clock. It's 5.14. Ohmigod. I forgot all about Sandee. She probably punched the cabdriver. I remember her telling me about a brawl she had back in Pittsburgh where, and

I quote, 'The bitch was lucky I didn't climb across the table and throw her into the wall.' Lucky indeed. Sandee is certainly a character and a fierce one at that. But she's a good woman. She makes me feel good, a feat few can accomplish.

I'm not too worried about Sandee's reaction. I stop thinking and just lie. Riley's next to me half asleep, stroking my hair. Some people are still talking downstairs. The noise doesn't bother me. I'm content. Wow, did I say that aloud? Content. Mark this day on your calendar, everybody. Gwen Bendler is satisfied. Hey, maybe it's the alcohol talking. But you know what the good part is... it probably isn't.